Woodlawn Cemetery

By
Charles F. Nearon

Copyright © 2007 by Charles F. Nearon

All rights reserved. No part of this book shall be reproduced or transmitted in any form or by any means, electronic, mechanical, magnetic, photographic including photocopying, recording or by any information storage and retrieval system, without prior written permission of the publisher. No patent liability is assumed with respect to the use of the information contained herein. Although every precaution has been taken in the preparation of this book, the publisher and author assume no responsibility for errors or omissions. Neither is any liability assumed for damages resulting from the use of the information contained herein.

This is a work of fiction. Names, characters, places, and incidents either are the product of the author's imagination or are used fictitiously. Any resemblance to actual events or locales or persons, living or dead, is entirely coincidental.

ISBN 0-7414-4281-7

Published by:

1094 New DeHaven Street, Suite 100
West Conshohocken, PA 19428-2713
Info@buybooksontheweb.com
www.buybooksontheweb.com
Toll-free (877) BUY BOOK
Local Phone (610) 941-9999
Fax (610) 941-9959

Printed in the United States of America

Printed on Recycled Paper

Published December 2007

This book is dedicated to my late wife Jeanne who insisted I try writing a book when I retired from the work world, who was there to encourage me, who proof read and edited, who pushed me when I got lazy and who loved me. I'm sorry my dearest Jeanne you are not here to see OUR work published. I love you.

Special thanks to my daughter Cheryl and my son Charles who read my early drafts and further encouraged me.

Thanks to my dear friend Salina who edited my manuscript and helped me in so many ways.

CAST OF CHARACTERS

Nelson Whitman   37 year old bachelor who is gliding through life with not much ambition until he meets

Dolores Lake   34 year old co worker of Nelson who has goals in life and falls in love with Nelson,

Sheila (pronounced SHAY_LA) Parks Richards Childhood friend of Nelson. They had a special non-physical love for each other.

Victoria Whitman Spivey   Nelson's sister

Walter Spivey   Victoria's husband

Linda Spivey   Daughter of Walter and Victoria

Lisa Porter   Sexy classmate of Nelson and Sheila, no morals, no conscience

Pete Hairston   Chief financial officer for Enright Industries. Greedy and dishonest.

Frank Richards   Sheila's husband, FBI agent

Bill Evans   Youngstown Ohio detective

Mr. Enright   CEO Enright Industries

Joe James   Dock Forman at Enright's

Mickey   Truck driver for Enright

Mark and Marilyn Decker   Walter Spivey's brother-in law and sister

Ken Decker   Mark and Marilyn's son

Willis Sharpe   Murdering son-in-law of

Arthur Kimble   Millionaire industrialist

Margaret Lake   Dolores' sister from Texas

Kathryn Kimble-Sharpe   Murdered wife of Willis Sharpe

Karen Van Horn   One time stripper and later famous actress and dear friend of Nelson and Dolores.

Sheila Whitman   Child of Nelson and Dolores

Woodlawn Cemetery exists and is a 470 acre plot in the Northeast Bronx in New York City. It is bordered on the North by East 233rd Street, on the East by Webster Avenue, on the south by Gun Hill Road and on the west by Jerome Avenue. We thank the board of Trustees for their permission to use the name.

The New York City subway system is real and all lines and stations are real. The Lexington Avenue line is as it was in the 1950's and 1960's.

City Island exists. It is a part of the Bronx, found in Eastchester Bay and features many fine seafood restaurants.

All the streets, avenues and drives in New York City that were mentioned, actually exist.

Horn and Hardart's and Bickfords were fast food restaurants in New York. Howard Johnson Restaurants were at the rest stops on the Pennsylvania Turnpike.

The *Youngstown Vind*icator is the real Newspaper for Youngstown Ohio.

The *New York Daily News* is real.

The City College of New York was known as CCNY in the 50's and 60's. It is now the City University of New York. Hunter College was a women's college in New York

There was a Roosevelt Hotel near 42nd Street and Lexington Avenue in New York. This is the Grand Central area

The Grand Central Station of the Post Office is real.

The Brown Derby was a chain of steak houses in Cleveland

The *Cleveland Press* was a real newspaper. It no longer exists.

The Hollenden House and Higbee's were a hotel and department store in Cleveland.

Except for Willie Mays, Mickey Mantle and President John F. Kennedy, all characters are fictitious

Remembrance, Ohio is fictitious. Bars, restaurants and lounges mentioned are fictitious.

Enright Industries is fictitious

WOODLAWN CEMETERY

PART 1

CHAPTER I

THE VISIT

Nelson Whitman was one of those WW II veterans that opted for the New York Post Office in 1945. It was a job that was immediately available and did not require special education or training. It also was a very secure job.

At the present time he has more than 14 years of service and is in a rut. He rents a room from his sister Victoria who, together with her husband, Walter, owns the house on East 231st Street in the Bronx, the only borough of New York City that is a part of the mainland, USA. He works the third tour as a clerk, sorting mail, at Grand Central Station, riding the subway to and from work. His workday ends at 12.30AM and he boards the East 241st Lexington Avenue express at 12:50 AM arriving at East 233rd Street at 1:35 AM. This had been his routine five days a week for several years. Occasionally he would stop at McMahon's, a bar and grill on Lexington Avenue frequented mostly by postal workers, for a beer and some camaraderie.

On the night Nelson decided to hang around for a while, Dolores Lake, a cute little single girl, with dark brown almond shaped penetrating eyes, was also at the bar. She was a fun loving person who laughed easily but was quite intelligent and had a serious side when she needed it. Nelson inched his six-foot frame past Dolores and up to the bar.

"Well...look who's here. What's with you Nelson?" Dolores asked, "You usually run out at 12:30 on the dot.

"I felt like hanging out for a while." Nelson replied. He was surprised she noticed when he left work. He thought she only saw him during work hours and forgot him completely when the day ended.

He worked up the courage and asked, "You want a beer?"

"Sure."

He knew Dolores for a few years but never really socialized with her. This was the first time he sat at a booth, just him and her and it was nice. Spending the rest of the night with her crossed his mind but he really didn't expect to. Other than sitting with him for a few minutes and enjoying the beer, Dolores indicated no real interest in furthering the relationship. Eventually she got up, thanked him, and mingled with the crowd. He glanced at his watch and noted it was nearly 1:30 AM.

"I guess I better get home," he silently told himself.

He walked the few blocks to the subway station feeling just slightly lightheaded from the three beers he had. Since he was off his routine, he didn't realize he boarded the Woodlawn train instead of the White Plains Road line.

Nelson fell asleep before the train reached 86th Street. He awoke with a start just as the train was leaving Mosholu Parkway.

"Damn," he said aloud. No one was offended because there was no one else in the car.

"Now I have to go all the way back to 149th Street. Damn it."

Woodlawn was the northern terminal of the Jerome Avenue line bordering the west side of Woodlawn Cemetery, a 470-acre plot established in the middle of the nineteenth century.

He glanced at his watch and noted it was 2:30 AM. It isn't unusual for a thick fog to form in the early morning hours in late May so Nelson barely noticed the mist creeping across the elevated tracks. As the train entered the mist Nelson did notice this was an unusually thick fog. He couldn't see the Woodlawn station at all. In fact he couldn't see the subway car in front of him, or any lights next to the train.

"I don't think this is ordinary fog," he thought, "Fog doesn't smell."

It was a heavy choking smell, not from gas or fire. It smelled like freshly turned earth, like a new grave.

Why isn't this thing slowing down? What's wrong with the motorman and where is the conductor? We must be entering the station by now and there's no more track after this.

The questions swirled around in Nelson's head as he attempted to see through the impenetrable mist. Rather than slowing, the train began to pick up speed. Nelson began to panic.

"God, we're going to crash into the barriers!"

He started to run towards the rear of the train the logic being, the last car will be cushioned against all the other cars. The train continued to pick up speed then suddenly there was no further sound from the motors and the clickety clack of the wheels on the tracks ceased. The mist seemed to be thinning as the train sped silently through…what?

There were no tracks, no landscapes, in fact there was now no train. Nelson was floating alone in the mist.

And then the mist disappeared and the green grass and white monuments and multi- colored trees and bushes appeared. Bright sunlight lit up Woodlawn Cemetery. Ordinarily this would have been a relief, but why was the sun blazing away at 3:00 AM?

The earthy odor was now gone but Nelson's confusion and bewilderment didn't fade away.

He was looking around, trying to see or hear someone, trying for an explanation when he heard, "Hi Nelson." He turned and saw a face he had never expected to see again.

"Sheila!" he exclaimed. (Her name was not pronounced in the usual form of SHEE-LA but as, SHAY-LA)

"It's really me Nelson. Remember that spring day we walked together through this cemetery?"

"Yes, I remember, it was the day I really fell in love with you."

"And I with you."

Sheila was a friend Nelson made back in the first grade. They remained friends all their lives even corresponding while Nelson was in the army. He always had a special place in his heart for her and was devastated when he heard she had died in an automobile accident. Obviously he was misinformed.

"I had heard..." Nelson hesitated, "I heard you were killed in an auto accident."

Sheila smiled and Nelson was so very glad the information he received a few years ago was incorrect.

****

FLASHBACK I

SHEILA

Sheila Parks joined Nelson's first grade class back in 1930, a few months after the regular school year had begun. Her parents had died and she was being raised by an uncle and aunt who had moved into the Bronx neighborhood from Manhattan.

Nelson was as smitten as a six year old could be when he first saw her. He was ecstatic when the teacher found her a desk right next to his.

They became good friends as the years passed working on school projects together, walking home together and simply enjoying each other's company. When they became teenagers they attended different high schools but they continued to see each other and as the pubescent hormones began to rise they saw each other in a different light. They really loved each other in a very special way. They were young, healthy maturing people and there were moments when the natural instincts of males and females arose. Sheila had turned sixteen the previous April and had just about reached her physical maturity. Nelson was about six months older but boys mature at a slower rate. He was still a gangly teenage boy whose arms were too long and whose feet were too big. They were strolling along Webster Avenue one balmy afternoon in May. "You want to walk through the cemetery?" Sheila asked. "My mother and father are buried here, we can visit their graves."

"That sounds like a good idea. It's real pretty in there in the spring."

They walked along the winding paths enjoying the aroma of spring flowers and freshly mown grass. Nelson was overcome with her loveliness. They touched hands and soon were in an embrace. Their lips met and Sheila's tongue flicked out against his. Nelson's hand slipped down over her buttocks and she pressed her pelvic area close. Then they suddenly moved apart. "Nelson," she whispered, "I love you too much to let this happen, and I think it's wrong. I don't want to get physical because we will lose something."

Nelson, although a normal young man who usually let his loins do his thinking, knew also he loved her too much to ruin their unique and beautiful relationship, a relationship of souls rather than bodies. "You're right," he told her, "Let's not destroy anything at this time. Maybe some day ..." In spite of his appearance, Nelson was able to think in a mature manner. "But Woodlawn cemetery will always have a special meaning."

"You know, I hope it does happen someday." Sheila

giggled, "I bet we could make some good looking kids."

They both laughed and the subject never came up again.

****

FLASHBACK II

THE CLASS OF 1938

In early July 1958, Nelson boarded the subway at his usual East 233rd Street station. He glanced at an abandoned New York Daily News sports page that trumpeted the American League All Star victory at Baltimore's Municipal Stadium. He was reading about Willie Mays' first pitch single when he was interrupted by a voice.

"How ya doing Nelson!"

Bobby Weston was in the same class in elementary school and went to the same high school as Nelson but they weren't close friends. They simply knew each other.

"Hey, Bobby, haven't seen you in years. What's going on?"

They talked about old times for a while. The conversation then turned to Sheila. "You remember Sheila Parks don't you?" Bobby asked.

"Of course I remember Sheila. Her name is Richards now, she married a guy named Frank Richards and moved to Ohio." Nelson said.

"You didn't hear? She was killed in an auto accident a couple of months ago. There was something fishy going on with her and her husband. He was FBI and got dirty. I think he was involved in dope. He was trying to escape and she was in the car. He ran into a bridge or something and she was killed. They found a whole bunch of dope at his house. He's in that federal prison in Pennsylvania now.

"That wasn't a good year for the class of 1938," Bobby went on, "Pete Hairston was found in a hotel room with his throat cut the next day. Remember Lisa Porter, the bimbo with the great ass? She disappeared. The police think she killed Pete."

Nelson's hair stood up on the back of his neck and his stomach began to churn. "Oh, man, I didn't know, Oh man. I kept saying I'd call them tomorrow and kept putting it off. How come I never read anything about them?"

"This happened in Ohio so there wasn't much mention of it in the New York papers."

The rest of the ride was in silence and Nelson barely heard Bobby say goodbye at the 59th Street station. When he arrived at 42nd Street Nelson decided not to work that night. He walked to a telephone booth, dropped his coin in the slot and dialed the timekeeper's office. "I won't be in tonight, I'm really pretty sick."

He crossed to the other side of the platform, the uptown side, and boarded the train back home. He went directly to his room, lay across his bed and just stared at the ceiling through tear-filled eyes. "Why the hell am I such a damn procrastinator," he asked himself over and over. "Now there is no tomorrow. Sheila, Sheila, I love you so much."

CHAPTER II

HOW LONG DOES A DREAM LAST?

"I am so glad your 'passing' was exaggerated." Nelson said with a chuckle.

Sheila smiled again and began moving towards him. It was a strange kind of motion. She didn't seem to be walking but rather, gliding along. "The report," Sheila said. "was not entirely exaggerated. Look at the tombstone in front of you."

It wasn't really a tombstone rather a plaque with words that seemed to be glowing, etched on the surface. Nelson eyes became the size of silver dollars. His mouth was agape as he read the wording on the simple monument.

SHEILA PARKS RICHARDS
April 17, 1924   February 22, 1958

Sheila wasn't buried in Woodlawn; Nelson would have known she died if she had been. However, Woodlawn Cemetery played a significant role in the lives of Sheila and Nelson. What the hell is going on? Dark clouds began to form in the bright blue sky and the greens and yellows of the landscape began to become less brilliant. Her eyes filled with tears and her voice was pleading. "Nelson, you've got to help me, you've got to!" Then, together with the plaque, she began to fade away.

The hiss of the closing subway door caused Nelson to awaken with a start. Just as the train was pulling out of the 125th Street station, he noticed the destination sign that read, *Woodlawn.* "Whoa," he told himself, "I'm on the wrong train!" He got up from his seat preparing to disembark at East 149th Street and change to the 241st Street train. What a weird dream, he thought, it sure was realistic though. His thoughts about his dream were suddenly interrupted when he felt the dampness on his shoes and saw the blades of wet grass clinging to his soles. Nelson was wide-awake for the half hour ride to the East 233rd Street station with thoughts of Sheila Parks and the wet grass on his shoes. He was exhausted by the time he arrived at his room and decided to forego his usual pre bed snack. His sister, Victoria, woke him at noon, and noticed he was still in his street clothes, sprawled across his bed.

"What's wrong?" Victoria asked, "You came in late last night and just plopped on your bed. Did you get bombed?"

"No, I wasn't bombed. I did stop for a beer after work and got on the Woodlawn train by mistake." Nelson continued, "I fell asleep and had the weirdest dream."

Ordinarily a dream begins to fade shortly after awakening. However this dream remained as vivid in his head as it was some nine hours ago. He and Victoria discussed it while Nelson ate the meal she had prepared for him. "I don't know what to say," Vicky said, "and I sure don't know where the grass on your shoe came from. You must have walked across somebody's lawn."

"Yeah, right. I walked across somebody's lawn between 125th Street and 149th Street, in the subway tunnel," he said sarcastically. They both decided not to pursue this issue any further…at this time.

He left the house at 2:30 and began his walk to the subway station. While he waited for the train, he glanced over the station railing and could see Woodlawn Cemetery a couple of blocks away. He was startled when he heard, "Nelson, help me." There was no one else on the platform at that time and little drops of sweat formed on his lip.

He looked to the right and the left and shook his head. "Geez," he said aloud, "How long does a dream last?"

****

FLASHBACK III

THE WAR EFFORT

When America entered World War II in 1941, Sheila and her childhood friend, Lisa Porter were in their senior year in High School. As it was for all Americans, life was going to be radically changed. Most of the boys they had grown up with would soon be in the military and young women would join the work force in what used to be men's jobs. Upon graduating in the summer of 1942, they decided to contribute to the war effort and postpone college. Besides, there was a whole bunch of money to be made. Lisa was fully developed by the time she was thirteen and knew how to take full advantage of the stammering and embarrassed teenage boys. She was glad to get a factory job because she would be around those men who couldn't make it into the service or who's jobs were of vital importance. By age 18, Lisa was blond and beautiful. Her 36-24-38 measurements would make some Hollywood types envious. She could start wearing those baggy slacks for women and she bought them a size too small to be sure to show off her gorgeous little fanny. She wore tight sweaters or blouses with the top two buttons undone. She always made sure there was considerable cleavage showing.

Sheila on the other hand was extremely conservative and quite serious. She truly wanted to contribute to the war effort and even considered joining the WAACS or WAVES. She had taken business courses in her senior year and could type 55 words a minute, Additionally, she was quite proficient in shorthand. She worked in the same factory as Lisa but in the administrative office.

Peter Hairston, another classmate from grammar school, had also taken business courses in High School including basic accounting.

He failed his physical due to a heart murmur and was classified in the draft as 4F. He joined the office staff at the factory in the fall of 1942.

Nelson was quite intelligent and able, but was rather lazy. He was content with any job that provided him with necessities and perhaps enough for a little fun. But he had no desire for fancy cars or clothes or large bank accounts.

After graduation Nelson got a job as an usher at a local movie house. When he had a night off, he would go to a bar and grill called Erwin's, frequented by the employees of the factory. They were a fun group and he also knew Sheila would be there from time to time. They still had that great relationship and enjoyed each other even more now that they were virtually adults.

Watching Lisa flaunt herself and act provocatively with the men, he asked Sheila, "How did you ever hook up with her? Your long time buddy is some bimbo."

"She's been like that since sixth grade. She used to leave her window shade up and undress knowing full well the boys next door were watching her. We played with dolls and things until we were about ten, then all she thought about was boys. She would take off all her clothes and stand in front of the mirror checking to see if her boobs were growing out and if any hair was growing down there." Sheila's eyes glanced down at her crotch area. "When she started talking about sex acts and if I knew how to 'do it', I didn't even know what she was talking about. I decided to end our friendship and I started drifting away from her then."

Nelson was drafted in 1943, attained the rank of sergeant and was sent to England as a part of the D-Day force.

In the meantime the factory in the North Bronx that had been a textile mill, was turning out parachutes made from the new synthetic material called Nylon. Lisa continued to flirt with the 4F's, those too old for the draft and the teenagers who were too young. Sheila was promoted to office manager and supervised a staff of five. Pete became the chief bookkeeper.

Sheila looked out of the office window one afternoon and noticed Pete talking with Lisa on the work floor. They seemed to be very involved in serious matters. Two or three times a day, Pete would leave the office and he would meet Lisa. Sometimes they exchanged what looked like envelopes.

Another time Sheila was returning from the ladies' room when she overhead Lisa saying,

"O K, I'll see you later when you have it."

Later that afternoon Sheila saw Lisa at Erwin's and casually asked, "What were you and Pete talking about near the exit door?"

"Oh, nothing", she answered, "Oh look at that cute guy who just came in. See ya later."

Sheila noticed the sudden change of subject and thought she glimpsed a moment of panic on Lisa face.

Sheila enjoyed a cocktail hour at Erwin's from time to time and also enjoyed engaging in little innocent flirtations. Eventually she became serious with a man who delivered material to the factory. His name was Frank and he was classified 1A in the draft, and in early 1944 the telegram came that opened with the words,

"Greetings from the President of the United States"

Sheila and Nelson had been corresponding while he was in the army. He received a letter one day that read as follows:

Dear Nels,

How is it going? I got your last letter and was really happy to hear from you. I keep praying for you and hope you stay safe. Remember keep your dopey head DOWN.

I'm still at the factory with Lisa and Pete but something looks funny. They are spending a lot of time together but I don't think they are dating. I see her at the bar from time to time with other men. Of course, she would be with other men

even if they were dating.

Oh well. Why should I care?

Now the big news. You know the Frank I wrote to you about? He got drafted and will be going away soon. He asked me to go with him. He wants to marry me.

You know you will always be my main love but I'm really crazy about this guy and I think I'll say yes.

Write when you get a chance.

Love you,

Sheila

Nelson wrote back to Sheila:

Dearest sweet Sheila,

I am truly happy for you. If this is the guy with whom you want to spend the rest of your life, go for it. You know I always loved you and I believe you loved me in the same way. But, except for that day at Woodlawn, we were never in love.

About Pete and Lisa, there was always something weird about them. I suggest you keep your distance and let them do whatever it is they're doing.

The letter continued with Nelson saying what he could about his time in England. Of course he wasn't allowed to say where he was, but she knew it was England and she knew eventually he would be part of the force to invade Europe, and she prayed daily for his safety.

****

CHAPTER II (CONTINUED)

Nelson was dozing off as the Lexington Avenue Express rattled its way into the tunnel at East 149th Street. He started when he felt someone touch his arm. He opened his eyes and he was on the Woodlawn Station platform completely alone. He glanced over the railing at the stones and monuments that seemed to be shimmering.

"What the hell?" he said aloud and jumped at the sound of his own voice in the dead silence.

"Nelson, there's something I need you to do," came a disembodied voice from the direction of the cemetery, "help Frank and me."

****

FLASHBACK IV

CLASS OF 1938

Frank Richards and Sheila were married in January 1944 and Frank was sent overseas in March. He made it through the war without a scratch and returned to his wife in late 1945. Frank used his G I Bill and enrolled in the City College of New York. Job opportunities were posted on a bulletin board and the one that interested Frank was for policemen in Ohio. He applied and was accepted for a position as patrolman in Remembrance, Ohio in early 1948. Sheila and Frank packed up and moved to the Buckeye State.

"We'll keep in touch," Sheila told Nelson at a going away party they held in their Manhattan apartment. Lisa and Pete also were at the party, Lisa doing her usual flirting with all single and most of the married men. Pete was also there but didn't do much socializing. He seemed to be trying to get

Lisa alone but it was difficult for her to pull away from the cadre of men surrounding her.

Pete and Lisa continued their work at the factory after the war which now was turning out fabrics made from nylon and other synthetic fibers and was owned by a corporation called, Enright Industries. Pete enrolled at CCNY and eventually passed his CPA exam. He was now chief financial officer for Enright Industries and Lisa was his secretary. Both seemed to be doing quite well financially, in fact, Nelson thought, better than what would be from the average salaries for each position.

Sheila berated Nelson on several occasions for not taking advantage of his abilities particularly in financial matters and he was well read in money matters. Nelson, as noted earlier, was on the lazy side and was content to continue as a postal clerk. He would nevertheless take the exam for foreman eventually.

Frank also had suspicions about Pete's and Lisa's life styles and when he saw him surreptitiously pass an envelope to her, his policeman's instincts kicked in.

"I'll miss you sweetheart," Nelson replied, "But I'm really glad for you and Frank."

They corresponded for a while with letters, then a birthday card and a Christmas Card only. Frank and Sheila both were working at jobs that gave them little time to visit New York. Except for a third cousin in Westport Connecticut, Frank had no family there and Sheila's uncle and aunt had both passed away therefore she had no reason to visit. Nelson on the other hand had several opportunities to go to Ohio but kept putting it off. Nelson never forgot her nor did she forget him, but they were now living on different planes.

Lisa Porter had two great loves, money and sex. While still in high school she sought out the boys who came from relatively comfortable backgrounds. She had the reputation for being easy and lost her virginity before she was sixteen. She also was responsible for helping at least five boys lose theirs by the time she was eighteen. But she didn't just give it away. There was considerable material gain from her lover d'jour. By the time she started work at Enright Industries, she had received a considerable settlement from one boyfriend's family when she claimed she was pregnant. She wasn't of course, but told the boy she had a miscarriage some three weeks after her settlement. Since money was her first love, even over sex, she was very careful about getting pregnant even in the days before birth control pills.

Peter Hairston was a serious minded financial type. He was able to figure money making enterprises, both legal and illegal. He had no particular loyalty to Enright Industries in spite of the generous way he was treated. He started right out of High School at a fair salary and received raises commensurate with his skills and increased responsibilities. But Pete was greedy and this would eventually cause his downfall and his life.

During the war, Enright Industries supplied the military with parachutes on a cost plus basis. The government would pay whatever costs were involved in providing the goods, plus a percentage for profit. Therefore it wasn't necessary for the business to be cost conscious. Pete padded payrolls and shipping costs through manipulation of the books and was able to pocket considerable sums without the knowledge of management.

Lisa was fiscally astute and figured out what Pete was doing. "Don't worry Petey boy," she told him, "I'm not going to turn you in unless…"

"Unless what?" Pete asked nervously.

"Um…unless you don't want to cut me in."

Pete cashed the government check one afternoon and

before returning to his office he stopped at Lisa's work station with an envelope. Lisa batted her eyes, rubbed her body up against him and glanced up to see Sheila looking out her office window at them.

There was another occasion where Pete couldn't get to the bank on time. He was walking down the corridor to the men's room passing Lisa along the way. He whispered to her, "I don't have the cash right now but I'll get it this afternoon and I'll see you before we close." Sheila exited the ladies room as Lisa replied to Pete, "O. K., I'll see you later when you have it."

After the war ended, Lisa attended secretarial school and graduated, at best, an average typist and stenographer. There were a few men in the class and they got to know Lisa quite well. She, however barely remembered their names.

Pete's workload required an assistant so he asked for a secretary.

"Do you have anybody in particular you would like to have?" Mr. Enright inquired.

"Lisa Porter just graduated from secretarial school and I've known her for a million years. I think she and I would work together pretty well."

"O.K. Pete, go ahead and hire her."

Pete wasn't particularly good looking or sexy but Lisa still loved sex. After a few drinks at Erwin's, she gave him a few signs which Pete recognized and by ten that evening they were in bed together. "Lisa, I've always wanted…"

Lisa cut him off. "Don't say anything you might want to take back later. You were good, you were a lot of fun and maybe we'll do this again. But there's not going to be any boyfriend-girlfriend thing going on. I'm going to sleep with lots of people and you should too."

They lay together quietly for a while finishing off the

proverbial after sex cigarettes.

Then Lisa said, "I've been thinking about making a lot of money-for both of us."

"How?"

"Remember the things we heard about prohibition? There was lots of money to be made from providing liquor to folks who would pay anything for it."

"But liquor's legal now. Why should anyone buy it illegally?"

"Not liquor Petey boy."

He hated when she called him that but he tolerated it for now anyway. She was a great help in both his legitimate and illegitimate enterprises.

"There's a big demand for stuff like marijuana, opium and other things. The mob controls it but they always need distributors. We could make a whole bunch of cash as long as we don't try to rip off the mob.

"I tried marijuana once and it made me pretty high. I remember having a great time with two dudes and another girl. But I really don't need to be high to have fun. I just love rolling in the sack with guys ...or girls."

Pete shuddered for a moment and glanced sideways at Lisa who was laying back smiling. He made a mental note that good as she was in bed, he'd better not get involved in her freaky sexual activities. He was glad she told him not to say anything he might want to take back later.

"But there are people," Lisa continued, "that need to be high and will pay anything for this dope and since we are shipping materials to Pennsylvania and Ohio we could take advantage of Enright's trucks and warehouses.

CHAPTER III

MORE THAN JUST A DREAM

Nelson felt something against his foot and jumped up as a walking passenger said, "Excuse me." The train was pulling out of the 125th street station and despite the swirling overhead fans he was sweating rather profusely. He looked at the destination sign which read, *Woodlawn.* "How can it be Woodlawn, I'm traveling downtown."

"Nelson help me put the evil witch called Lisa where she belongs." rang clearly in his head. It sounded so real, he thought, what is happening to me? What happened to Sheila?

He decided then that as soon as possible he was going to do some research about Sheila's death and Frank's incarceration. The train pulled into 42nd Street, the destination sign now correctly reading, *Utica Ave.* and Nelson exited and began walking to his job. He started to think there is more than just a dream going on, I'm getting some kind of message.

****

FLASHBACK V

FBI

Frank and Lisa moved to Remembrance, Ohio where he began his job as a patrolman. Remembrance wasn't exactly a high crime area being a quiet rural village. The village abutted a lake which was large enough for a beach and some small boats. During the summer there was a considerable amount of traffic in the area as well as some minor crime such as disturbing the peace, public drinking, illegal parking and such. Frank became one of the better liked members of the department enforcing the laws fairly. He took some law courses at the local college at night and when he saw an announcement about applications for the FBI, he was quick to respond.

Although they tried, Sheila did not become pregnant and eventually she got a job in a law office. She attached a note to the Christmas card she sent to Nelson.

Things are going pretty good for us here in Ohio. We miss you a lot. Frank got accepted by the FBI and starts training in January. He has to go to Washington so we might come to New York for a couple of days. I got a raise at the law firm and really like what I'm doing. Have a great Christmas and New Year.

Love,

Sheila

Nelson read the card over a couple of times and thought how nice it will be to see Sheila again. But Sheila came down with the flu just after the holidays and couldn't make it to New York. Frank wanted to stay home with her but she told him, "You have to start your training, you never know when they'll be starting a new class."

"But I won't be stopping in New York," he said.

"Why not?" Sheila protested, "I'll be OK and Mrs. Cochran next door said she'd look in on me. Go see Nelson, then go get trained. I'll be waiting for you."

CHAPTER IV

DOLORES

When he got to work and was seated at his position sorting mail into the many pigeon holes in front of him, Dolores, the pretty lady he had a beer with a few nights ago, came in and sat next to him.

"Hey, Nelson, how's it going?"

At first Nelson didn't realize she was sitting there and didn't answer.

"Hey" Dolores snapped, "You mad at me or something?"

Nelson looked at her and answered, "Oh, sorry, I was thinking about something. I never could be mad at you."

"You better not be," she said with a smile.

Dolores' purse was open and Nelson noticed a small pamphlet with the word, DREAM on the cover.

"What's the dream book about? You trying to hit the number?"

"Oh this." A somber look replaced the usual twinkle in her eye.

"There are some interesting things you can learn in these little pamphlets. I've had some strange dreams and I'm trying to find out what they mean."

Nelson thought for a while then decided it was time he tried to find out what his dreams meant. She's single, I'm single, there's no impropriety in our going somewhere together.

"Would you like to go with me to McMahon's after work?" Nelson asked, "I'd like to talk about dreams and what they might mean."

"Hmmm, a good serious discussion. I'd like that. You got a date buster."

They walked together into McMahon's at 12:35 and found a booth near the kitchen. Nelson went to the bar and returned with two draught beers. It was a relatively quiet night so they were mostly undisturbed. A few of their co-workers happened by and said hello. No one really cared who came in with whom.

Dolores sipped her beer and asked, "So, what kind of dreams are you having?"

"Well, you know I live in the northeast Bronx," Nelson answered and before he could continue she said, "No, I didn't."

"Of course, why should you? Anyway, I take the White Plains Road line home but remember the night we had a beer here?"

"Yes, I was surprised to see you. I enjoyed sitting with you."

"Yeah, me too. When I left here I was a little light headed and didn't notice I got on the Woodlawn train. I dozed off and woke-at least I thought I woke up-as we left the next to last stop on that line. We never arrived at the last station."

He continued the story telling Dolores about the mist, the sun shine, the floating tombstone and the meeting with Sheila.

"Who is Sheila?" she inquired.

Nelson explained and then told of his awakening in time to transfer to the correct train.

Dolores began to speak. "Dreams of cemeteries and dead people usually indicate some unfinished business that needs finalizing. Did you and Sheila have a thing that didn't work out?"

"No, we were best friends since grammar school and even though I always loved her, we never were in love. We kissed as friends kiss from time to time except once, when we let our 'animal instincts' take over. She was gorgeous, you know."

"Did you resent her marrying someone else?"

"No, I was glad for her and Frank became a good friend of mine."

"What about her leaving the state? Did that bother you."

"I missed her, I still miss her, but she had her life and I had mine. I wanted to go to Ohio a few times to see them but I kept putting it off."

"That could be the unfinished business."

They sat in the booth silently for a while. "Do you believe her husband was dirty?"

"Not really. I'm planning to do a little investigating on my own."

Then Nelson intrigued Dolores when he said, "I forgot to tell you. After that first dream, when I woke up I had wet shoes with little pieces of grass clinging to them."

"Oh boy. We need to get into this further. I don't think you were dreaming."

"What are you saying? You think I'm going nuts?

"No, no, not at all. I believe in spirits that have not yet let go of their earthly existence. Sometimes they don't know they're dead. Sometimes they know they're dead but have something to do before they leave. Not many people can communicate with them but you seem to be one who can."

"Last call!" McMahon yelled, and Nelson was surprised when he saw his watch read 2:45AM. "Do you want me to take you home?" he asked Dolores not expecting her to accept the offer (and secretly hoping she wouldn't because his mind now was on getting to the library and starting his investigation.)

"Not this time, but I'll see you tomorrow. Maybe we can continue this then."

Dolores hailed a cab and took off up Lexington Avenue. Nelson had no idea where she lived. He walked down to the subway station and made sure he boarded the 241st Street train. He stayed awake the whole time thinking about his dreams, his "date" with Dolores, and his anticipated future dates.

Nelson didn't get to bed until near 5:00AM but he was up and dressed by ten.

"What are you doing up already?" Victoria asked as she cleared away the breakfast dishes left by her husband and daughter.

"I need to go somewhere today. You got any coffee left?"

"You want breakfast? Where are you going?"

"No, thanks, I want to do some research at the library before I go to work. I'll get something at Bickford's when I get downtown."

As he sipped his coffee, Nelson said to Vicky, "You know those dreams I told you about? I think there's something more happening. I'm getting some kind of message."

Victoria waved her hands in the air and wailed, "*Ooohweeeoooh*"

"I'm not making fun of you Nelson but ghostly messages from beyond?"

Nelson realized how foolish he might sound. The sudden shifts to Woodlawn, the voice coming out of the dark, all could be imagination or a dream, but how do you explain the damp shoes and grass?

****

FLASHBACK VI

THAT UNFORGETTABLE BUTT

Frank stopped in New York on his way to Washington D C. He and Nelson got together at the Roosevelt Hotel in the Grand Central area. They stopped off at the bar while waiting for their table at an upscale eatery.

"You taking good care of my girl?" Nelson asked.

"Oh yes! She's the best thing that ever happened to me."

They were distracted by a group of people who entered the restaurant with relatively loud talking and much laughter. In the midst of several formally attired men with a dark mink jacket slung over her shoulders appeared a vaguely familiar face.

"Frank, Nelson," Lisa Porter shrieked, "what are you guys doing here?"

Her hair, her eyes, her lips were all professionally made up and except for the considerable cleavage showing, Nelson hardly recognized her. She was in fact quite beautiful. "Frank was in town," Nelson replied, "We thought we'd get together. This is a pretty good joint to get a beer."

"Would you like to join us?" Lisa could be very charming.

"Thanks but no thanks" Nelson answered, "But you and your party could join us here at the bar."

Lisa called out to her party, "I'll meet you guys in the dining room. I want to talk to my old friends here." They all moved from the bar to a booth after Nelson ordered an Old Fashion for Lisa and another beer for himself and Frank.

"So, Frank, what brings you back from the frontier?" Lisa asked.

Frank was a little annoyed with New Yorkers who thought the only civilized part of The United States was New York City but he said nothing.

"I'm on my way to Virginia to FBI training school."

"FBI! How exciting!" Lisa said, genuinely surprised. "What does Sheila think of that, and how is my old friend?"

"Sheila's fine and she's also fine with my career choice. She was going to come to New York for a couple of days but she came down with the flu." Frank thought to himself, why am I telling her all this, I don't even like this broad.

Nelson thought he saw Lisa move a little closer to Frank with a new twinkle in her eye and an extra wiggle to her butt.

"Table for Whitman is ready," came the announcement from the dining room. Both Frank and Nelson were relieved to get away from Lisa. "It was good seeing you guys again", Lisa exclaimed, "hope to see you again soon."

They all walked to the dining room together but Lisa turned to the right with a, "Bye bye!" and walked towards her party's table with an exaggerated swing to her unforgettable butt. After they were seated, Nelson and Frank looked at each other and began to laugh. "She's really a good looking babe but I'm afraid of her. She got the scariest eyes I ever saw." Nelson said. "I noticed she was making a move on you."

Frank nodded. "She's up to no good. She's seems to have a lot more money than a secretarial job would provide."

"She could be a high priced call girl," Nelson volunteered, "But why would she hang on to that secretary job? I saw Pete not so long ago and he told me she stills works for him."

"She and Pete are together in some kind of action, probably illegal."

"You're probably right but who gives a damn? They're not stealing my money."

"Yet" Frank added.

CHAPTER V

THE DATE

Nelson arrived downtown before noon and went directly to the public library on 42nd Street and Fifth Avenue. He approached the information desk and asked about out-of-town newspapers of 1958.

"Those papers are on micro-film. Go to that booth over there and someone will bring you the films. Do you know how to use the reader?"

"I guess I can figure it out."

After Frank completed his training for the FBI, he was assigned to the Cleveland office. Nelson asked for the Cleveland newspapers for 1958. He began leafing through the Cleveland Press looking for anything relating to drugs, shoot outs, and auto fatalities. He then saw a headline on February 23, 1958 announcing the injury to an FBI agent suspected of selling drugs.

An accident on Superior Avenue resulted in the death of a woman and a critically injured FBI agent. The agent was being chased by a deputy Sheriff who wanted to question him about drug traffic.

Before he could read further, he glanced at the clock on the wall and saw it was 3:30 PM.

He called to the librarian to take back the film saying, "I'll see you tomorrow."

Nelson went directly to his work site looking for Dolores. He spied her at her case, sorting the mail in a nonchalant manner. Another clerk was seated next to her and Nelson asked him to move over one spot. "I really need to talk to Dolores, man."

"No problem Nels, She ain't talking much anyway."

"I'm sorry," Dolores said to the clerk, "but I don't talk to ugly men."

The gentleman moved over with a smile. Dolores was a very sweet lady and if she insulted you, it wasn't taken seriously. If she didn't like someone she simply ignored him or her.

"I was at the library this afternoon," Nelson stated after he had settled in and began sorting the tray of letters in front of him, "and found an article in the Cleveland paper about Frank Richards and the accident where Sheila was killed."

Dolores' interest perked. "I've been thinking about your story and I've been doing some research myself. I read something about the paranormal. Sheila was killed before her time and she refuses to give up. She might have a need to tell you something."

Nelson wanted to talk more with Dolores but in a more private setting. One couldn't get into a really serious subject while on the work floor. "Would you like to go out with me to dinner sometime?" he asked.

Dolores was not completely surprised at the question. She noticed last night at McMahon's Nelson was kind of interested in a relationship. "Sure, I'd like that. When?"

"How about Saturday night? We could go to Horn & Hardarts..." Before he could complete the sentence, Dolores interrupted, "Horn & Hardarts? Are you crazy? This is going to be a real date where you pick me up and everything AND you have to wear a tie!"

"Hah, I was just kidding. I thought maybe we could go out to City Island for a good lobster dinner."

"I'd love to have dinner with you, Nelson."

Nelson was on his way home from work at about 1:15 AM Saturday morning. He was off for the weekend and was starting a short vacation on Monday. He was looking forward to his date with Dolores. The only other passenger in the car exited at Gun Hill Road and Nelson stared out the window at the passing light poles and buildings on White Plains Avenue. Then suddenly the scene changed to Woodlawn Cemetery. He was startled when he heard his name called and looked up to see Sheila Parks Richardson standing in front of him. "Sheila, is it you?"

"It really is me, Nelson, and I am dead. I can help you find the truth about Frank and put the witch away." Then she was silent but she smiled at him and slowly dissolved into nothingness while the scene returned to White Plains Avenue.

He banged his hands against his thighs, pinched his fingers and dug his nails into his palms as he clenched his fists. "Jesus God," he mumbled, "I know I'm not dreaming now. I know I'm awake! Sheila, where are you?"

The train pulled into the East 233rd Street station and Nelson pulled himself together enough to know where he was. He detrained and started his walk to his sister's house.

Looking left and right and turning around a few times, Nelson thought how much he would like to see Sheila. He wasn't afraid of her ghost, he knew she wouldn't harm him.

"I know I saw her, I was not dreaming" he told the empty street.

He awoke about 9:00 AM to the sound of Elmer Fudd, "Be vewy, vewy quiet! We're hunting Wabbits!" His eight year old niece was watching the Bugs Bunny show in the living room down stairs. "Turn that down a little," he heard his sister say, "Uncle Nelson is trying to sleep."

Nelson put on his robe and descended the stairs to the kitchen passing the living room on the way. "You keep blasting that thing, knuckle head, I'm moving out," he teased.

Linda ran to him and pulled on the sleeve of his robe, "No you are not! You are never NEVER leaving me!"

"OK, when you get married, I'm going on the honeymoon with you and living with you and your husband."

"I'm not getting married!" Linda squealed, "I hate boys...except you."

"Morning Vicky," Nelson said to his sister, "You have any coffee left?"

He sat down at the kitchen table and Victoria placed a cup of coffee in front of him.

"Where's Walter?"

Walter Spivey and Victoria Whitman were married in 1950 and Linda was born in 1952. They bought the house on East 231st Street in 1955. Nelson had a tiny apartment in Manhattan after he returned from the war. The apartment wasn't very pleasant and the neighborhood was deteriorating. There was a nice sized room above the front entrance to Victoria's house. It afforded Nelson the privacy he needed and since he had full kitchen privileges, he was glad to rent it and Walter appreciated the help with expenses.

Nelson bought a Ford sedan in 1955 but only used it on weekends. It was far too much trouble to drive to downtown New York and parking was virtually impossible. It did get a good workout on his off days and during the summer, he would take Linda to the beach or the parks or the zoo.

Tonight he was going to City Island on a date with Dolores who he found to be more and more desirable. He discovered she lived in a nice apartment on East 80th street and was supposed to pick her up there at 7:00PM.

"Walter went to the office this morning. He should be home around two." Victoria replied.

"I wonder if I could borrow that tan sport jacket of his.

I've got a date for tonight."

"A date!" Victoria said with amazement. "Who have you got a date with?"

"You don't know her, she's somebody I know from work. Her name is Dolores and maybe if you're good, you'll get to meet her."

Victoria poured coffee for Nelson and herself and sat down at the table with him. They discussed Dolores for a time and when Nelson mentioned she was interested in the paranormal, Victoria asked, "Does she know about your dreams?"

"We discussed them, in fact we're going out to tonight so we can talk more about this stuff.

"I have to spend more time at the library" Nelson continued, "I found an article about Frank being chased by the Ohio police and crashing into an overpass. He was arrested for accepting bribes and drug possession. I can't believe he was a dirty agent."

"I didn't know him that well," Victoria added, "but if Sheila thought he was OK, he was OK. I think he was set up."

Nelson was supposed to pick up Dolores around 7 PM this evening so he decided to go down town to buy some decent clothes-AND a tie. He picked out a silk tie with a ten dollar price tag on it, a tidy sum for the time.

****

FLASHBACK VII

ABSOLUTELY NO CONSCIENCE

Pete and Lisa had been using the factory as a distribution

point for their drug business. Having gained Mr. Enright's confidence, they pretty much were on their own as far as access to the building and equipment usage. They hired their own watchman who was instructed to look the other way, for which he was well compensated. Through manipulation of the books, Pete was able to have two watchmen on the payroll although only one body was in fact present.

"Don't ask any questions," Lisa told him, her cold unblinking eyes fixed on his, "and your tax free money will be here each week. Open your mouth to anyone and you can count on a nice long nap in New Jersey."

Lisa was a very forceful person and indicated she would not let anything get in the way of her activities, money making or sex. She was a little frightening the way she stared through people.

There was the time she picked up a good looking guy at the bar and followed him home in her own car. She didn't expect or even want him to take her home the next morning. All she wanted was some sex. He thought he could use her for his own pleasure then kick her out of bed telling her, "get lost bitch."

Lisa, a great actress, showed how hurt she was by sobbing as she slowly dressed even though she had used him for her own pleasure.

"Shut the hell up and get out of here." The man said, as he lay back and began to doze.

Lisa waited until he was fully asleep, then took her three inch stiletto heel and pounded it into his eyes. When he awoke screaming, blood pouring from his wounds, she smashed a lamp against his head, rendering him unconscious. She dragged his body, she was extremely strong for a woman, to the second floor window and pushed him out. She then collected her belongings and calmly strolled out of the building. She waited at the door for a few minutes to make sure no lights went on anywhere. Silently slipping into her car, she released the brake and let it coast without lights to the end of the street. Well away from the lover's house, and again making sure there were no other cars or pedestrians around, she started her engine, turned on her lights and drove home. She removed all her clothes including underwear and packed them in a paper bag. She then showered thoroughly put on her night clothes and robe, She carried the bag to the building incinerator, dropped it in, then calmly walked back to her apartment, turned out the light, got into bed and was asleep within minutes.

The lover, she never knew his name, did not die, but was blinded for the rest of his life and unable to speak or remember any of his past because of his brain damage.

****

FLASHBACK VIII

INTENT TO DISTRIBUTE

Their operation was expanding and with the unwitting assistance from Enright drivers, the drugs were transported with Enright's fabrics to Harrisburg and Pittsburgh Pennsylvania, and Youngstown, Ohio. Both Pete and Lisa were netting more than $2,000 a week, a handsome sum at the time, but Pete wanted more. The organized crime syndicate received the drugs from South America and Mexico and sent them to New York. Pete set up the system of receiving, packing and shipping them out and for this, they were paid 25% of the drug's value. Lisa was satisfied with her share and she knew it would increase as time went by. Besides, she rarely had to pay for things like jewelry, trips to Florida or Las Vegas or the Caribbean. One of her wealthy paramours, a married Wall Street executive, gave her a new Oldsmobile when she implied his wife could find out about them. She had more than $100,000 stashed away in several bank accounts. Pete on the other hand didn't think he netted enough from the weekly take. He tried to convince Lisa they should protest.

"Protest? To the mob? You aren't too bright are you Petey?" Lisa shook her head. "They'll negotiate only you won't hear their side because your ass will be rotting in a swamp somewhere in Jersey."

Enright Industries was expanding nationwide. The fabric business was doing quite well and with shopping centers popping up all over fabric stores were becoming the rage.

This was perfect for the drug operation. Mr. Enright was a brilliant businessman but he trusted people too much. He was proud of his chief financial officer who began as a bookkeeper during the war. He was totally unaware of Pete's other life because Pete kept the business financially sound and so far was able to hide many illegal fiscal transactions from the auditors. Trucks with license plates from Florida, Texas, South Carolina and Louisiana would arrive at the factory two or three times a month late at night and unload crates marked *synthetic fibers.* Pete was always there supervising the unloading while the watchman checked the opposite side of the building.

The following day Pete was on the dock with a clipboard marking the bolts of cloth being shipped to Pennsylvania and Ohio. The dock foreman wondered why Pete was there and asked him one day.

"You do your job," Pete growled, "and don't worry about mine."

CHAPTER VI

THE DATE (CONTINUED)

Nelson found a parking spot about a block away from Dolores' apartment house. He checked his brand new neck tie in the rear view mirror. Satisfied, he began his walk to her apartment and a smile began to form on his face as he tried to imagine how she would look and smell. Nelson really was looking forward to this date.

He was sure the whole building heard him gasp when Dolores opened her door. Of course, it was a silent gasp only Nelson could hear but she was absolutely beautiful. She wore a kind of purple colored blouse held up by those little spaghetti like straps. Her skirt was black and fit tightly across her hips revealing the elegant curve of her bottom. Her eyes sparkled and her lips were ruby red with a sheen to them Nelson had only seen in movies. Her brown hair had honey colored highlights and was somehow twirled up on her head. Little pearls dangled from her ears on almost invisible golden chains and around her neck was a string of half black and half white pearls.

Nelson couldn't hold it back any longer. "You're beautiful," he blurted out.

"Why thank you Nelson," she answered, "You aren't half bad yourself. Love your jacket.

Make yourself at home while I gather my stuff and we can be on our way." She disappeared into another room while Nelson took in the tasteful manner in which her apartment was furnished.

Dolores reappeared with a white sweater across her shoulders held together by a little chain and a tiny purse covered in some glittery stuff. "Let's go Mr. Whitman, I'm ready for nice juicy lobster tail."

****

FLASHBACK IX

DRUG SHIPMENT

Pete received a very large shipment of marijuana and heroin from New Orleans the previous night. Half the "bolts" of cloth that were loaded into Enright trucks for Northeast Ohio, were in fact hollow tubes in which close to one million dollars worth of drugs were packed. Pete wasn't taking any chances so he supervised the loading that day.

He also took some time off so he could follow the truck to Youngstown. He didn't want the drivers to see him so he installed an electronic tracking device on the truck the previous night. Lisa was aware of the value of the cargo and demanded she ride along with him. This wasn't such a bad idea since someone needed to listen to the signal from the truck.

"There'll be a constant beeping noise that will get louder as we get closer. Conversely, it will get softer as we get further away," he instructed Lisa.

"I kind of figured that. What happens if it stops beeping?"

"It means we lost the truck and this better not happen."

The dock foreman was miffed by Pete's attitude that morning and began thinking that there's something fishy going on here. Joe James, the foreman, knew Frank back when he was delivering materials during the war and knew he had become an FBI agent in Ohio. They hadn't kept in touch over the years but Joe could look him up.

After the truck left the factory, Joe called the local FBI office and asked how he could contact an agent.

"For what purpose?" the voice on the telephone asked.

"He was a good friend of my cousin who passed away recently and I thought he would like to know," Joe lied.

"We have an agent in the Cleveland Ohio office by that name. I suggest you call the Cleveland office and ask them if you can contact him."

"Thank you very much. That J Edgar Hoover is a hell of a fighter."

Joe heard a loud guffaw just before the line was disconnected.

After several calls were made back and forth, Joe's phone rang at his home.

"Hello? This is Frank Richards. I understand someone there wants to talk to me."

"Frank! This is Joe James from Enright's. I was on the dock when you use to deliver stuff here during the war."

"Yeah, yeah, I remember you Joe. How's it going? What's this about your cousin?"

Joe explained it was just an excuse to have the FBI office in New York locate him. There was no cousin or anything.

"You remember Pete Hairston?" Joe asked.

"Yeah."

"Well, he's a big shot here now, chief financial officer. Now, why would the financial officer be interested in shipping and receiving? Every so often, he's down here supervising the loading of the trucks, particularly those going to Pittsburgh and Youngstown."

"Maybe he needs to be sure about shipments,." Frank offered.

"I didn't think about it before, but it seems some trucks come in here at night. I noticed some fresh oil spots where none of our trucks have been."

"I'll look into it Joe," Frank promised, "it sounds like some kind of smuggling operation."

Lisa was lying on the back seat of the car listening to the beeping sound with her legs bent at the knee and a considerable amount of thigh and beyond, visible. She caught Pete stealing a look at her through the rear view mirror and said, "You like what you see Petey boy? Keep your eyes on the road. There'll be plenty to see later."

Pete was thinking about how he tried to stay clear of her crazy sex activities but she was so damn hot he only thought of how much he would like to jump this broad when she suddenly cried out, "The beeping's getting louder."

"He probably pulled into a rest stop. I think there's one about two miles ahead."

They pulled into the rest stop a couple of minutes later and saw parked in the truck area the big rig with the Enright logo on the side. "We may as well get some dinner now," Pete suggested. He let Lisa out at the restaurant door and proceeded to the gas pumps.

"What if he sees us?" Lisa asked before exiting the car.

"He probably doesn't know who we are. The drivers never come in the office."

Lisa was already seated at a booth in the Howard Johnson restaurant with a cup of coffee set in front of her when Pete entered the building. Mickey, the driver, was at the counter flirting with a buxom waitress. He may have looked at Pete but gave no sign of recognition. Pete went to the booth and ordered dinner. He sat so he could keep his eye on Mickey.

After about an hour, Mickey ended his "romance" with Big Boobs Bertha with, "I'll see you on the way back, baby."

"I can't wait Tiger," she answered with a hearty laugh.

Pete told Lisa they would wait about thirty minutes and then continue the journey.

Mickey was cruising along at 60 miles per hour about ten miles from the Ohio line.

A black Plymouth tore passed him moving in an erratic

manner. It drifted left and hit the median curb, bounced back into the passing lane. The driver who had dozed at the wheel hit his brakes. This caused the car to swerve out of control into Mickey's lane and Mickey instinctively stamped on his brakes. The truck slipped on to the right berm but hadn't slowed enough to avoid hitting the Plymouth which was knocked into a ravine. Mickey stopped the truck about a thousand feet down the road. He jumped from the cab and ran back to the overturned sedan where he could see the driver was severely injured if not dead.

"Oh oh," Lisa exclaimed, "the beeping is getting stronger."

"He slowed down or stopped," Pete mused, "I wonder why? There aren't any more stops before the Ohio border."

The red tail lights of the cars ahead began to light up and the traffic slowed. In the distance a siren was heard and within a few minutes, a state police car passed the now stopped traffic, on the left shoulder.

The traffic crept forward and eventually they saw the flashing emergency lights of the police cars. "Damn," Pete said, "that's our truck off to the side."

"Should we stop?" Lisa asked.

"No, somebody will want to know why."

"What are we going to do?"

Pete watched for an emergency stop cut on the right berm and found one about a half mile past the accident. He pulled over and waited. After about fifteen minutes an ambulance roared past, the siren wailing. Following was a state police cruiser and then, with a dented bumper, the familiar Enright logo on an eighteen wheeler.

"Supposing the truck had been wrecked and they found the stuff in there," Lisa wondered.

"I never even thought about the truck wrecking on the highway. We're going to need a contingency plan."

CHAPTER VII

CITY ISLAND

Nelson held the door as Dolores slipped into the passenger seat. He noticed she reached across to unlock his door as he walked around to the driver's side. "She smells delicious," he thought.

As soon as they turned the corner and headed for FDR Drive, Dolores asked, "Any more encounters, Nels?"

"She appeared in front of me when I was coming home this morning."

"Did she say anything?"

He told her about Sheila's appearance in the empty subway car and the message about putting Lisa away.

"I believe she is a ghost - not an evil or bad thing," Dolores said, "and she needs to finish something." Then she added, "or she might be warning you of something."

"I don't know what to think. Ghosts, spirits spooks, I never thought much about them."

"Do you believe there is a God?" she asked.

"Yeah, I guess."

"Well, He's a spirit, in fact we've been taught there is a Holy Ghost and no one ever thinks that's spooky. I don't think death is the end. We continue on another plane but sometimes we can't pass to that other plane until we finish something."

Changing the subject, Nelson said, "I stopped at the library this afternoon and found the article in the Cleveland paper about the accident that killed Sheila. It said the cops found six grand in cash and two k's of pot in Frank's garage. I don't believe it." Nelson's brow knitted and there was anger in his voice. "That god dam bitch had something to do with this." He apologized for his language but Dolores was

40

not shocked or offended.

They were silent as they drove north on the FDR drive, crossed into the Bronx and continued on to City Island. Turning into the parking lot of Angelo's, they found a spot not too far from the entrance and Nelson ran around to open the door for Dolores. They walked to the entrance and heads turned as she glided past. The duo made an extremely handsome couple.

****

FLASHBACK X

YOUNGSTOWN

Pete and Lisa arrived in Youngstown late in the evening. The truck had arrived at the warehouse but because of the hour, the unloading would wait until morning. A representative of the mob met them at a pre-selected hotel to discuss the finances.

"We need to unload the stuff before the day crew comes on," Pete announced

It was nearly midnight when Pete, Lisa and a special crew that was told to unload certain bolts of cloth and to ask no questions, arrived at the warehouse dock. On an earlier trip a curious laborer opened one of the bolts and discovered the plastic bags inside. He asked Lisa what was in the plastic bags and she replied, "Oh forget about the bags, get in the car with me."She lay on the back seat, her legs bent at the knee and her skirt pulled up to her hips. This inquisitive gentleman didn't return home that morning and was never seen again.

A rented truck pulled up to the Enright truck and specially marked bolts of cloth were transferred from the one to the other. A black Lincoln was idling nearby. The rear window rolled down and Pete was summoned. He was handed a small suitcase as the rented truck drove off and the mob official touched his index finger to his hat to Lisa and nodded to Pete, then disappeared into the night.

"Let's go!" Lisa excitedly said to Pete. They drove to the hotel, registered as husband and wife and went to their room.

"Open the bag, Petey my man," hollered Lisa, "I want to see what a quarter million dollars looks like."

Lisa was becoming visible excited. She unbuttoned her blouse, removed it and tossed it aside. She unzipped her skirt and let it drop to the floor Pete opened the bag and Lisa squealed. "Spread it out on the bed!" she panted as she removed her bra and slipped out of her panties. "Get your clothes off, quick." she ordered, "I want to screw on top of this money!" She was totally naked and lying atop countless $100 bills, her legs spread wide eager to admit Pete who was becoming a little frightened. She was so well lubricated, he slipped right into her and within a few minutes she reached climax, even before Pete ejaculated.

Her heart beat must have reached 130 per minute but was now starting to cool down. She really didn't need Pete in fact wasn't even aware of him on her. As soon as her bare skin touched the money she was ready for orgasm. Lisa's two favorite things, money and sex, came together and the sensation was indescribable.

Pete lit cigarettes for both of them, trying to be cool, and they lay there quietly for a while. Pete was becoming sleepy and extinguished his cigarette. He turned on his side, still nude and still on top of the money and drifted off. Lisa squirmed around over the money, rubbing it all over herself. She had lost her virginity more than twenty years ago but never had a sexual sensation like this one. She didn't need Pete for the next two orgasms she had.

The next morning Pete awoke to find the money neatly stacked and Lisa clad only in her panties seated at the little table. "There's exactly $249,800 here."

"Didn't you sleep last night?" he asked.

"No, I wanted to count the money. Go take a shower and get some clothes on. You look like crap naked."

Frank Richards was aware of the shipment from Enright to Youngstown. He told his superior he had some information about a possible drug deal going down and the transportation across state lines of a controlled substance. This made it an FBI matter. He knew about the distribution point of fabrics to Pittsburgh, Cleveland and Akron and drove to the Youngstown warehouse. The Enright truck was about 95% unloaded when Frank arrived and he noticed Mickey the driver counting the bolts of cloth and looking puzzled. Approaching Mickey, Frank said, "You drive for Enright? I used to deliver there during the war. Are they still located in the Bronx?"

"Yup," Mickey replied, "Same old place but it's a lot bigger now."

"Frank Richards," Frank said, extending his hand. Mickey accepted the hand and responded with a firm grip. "You look like something's bothering you,"

"I could have sworn I had a bigger load than that."

Frank walked around the dock with Mickey and stopped when he noticed a tire track next to the Enright truck. "Look at that." He said to the driver. "That tire was too small for an eighteen wheeler. Any other trucks come in this morning?"

"I don't know," Mickey answered, "Maybe the dock foreman knows."

Frank asked the foreman who told him Enright's truck came in late last night but nothing else was scheduled until this afternoon.

"There was another truck here, a smaller truck, because that track was made less than twelve hours ago. It rained last night you know but it stopped around midnight."

"When do you expect another truck from Enright?" Frank asked the foreman.

"Next Wednesday. They usually get here in the evening so we don't start unloading until morning."

Frank was in his car driving towards the Ohio Turnpike when he passed a downtown hotel and noticed a man and women getting into a 1957 Cadillac. He couldn't miss the skin tight skirt barely concealing a very familiar butt. It had been a few years since the meeting at the restaurant but Frank couldn't forget that undulating bottom walking into the dining room. He still didn't like this "broad" but he did like the way her ass looked. "That's Lisa Porter and the guy must be Pete Hairston," he told himself, "what the hell are they doing here?"

He returned to his Cleveland office and told his superior what he found in Youngstown.

"Something is going down at that warehouse and I'd like to stake it out."

Since the FBI was investigating drug smuggling at that time, the agent in charge decided this was part of their investigation and was glad to assign Frank to this case.

Frank returned home and told Sheila about seeing Lisa and Pete and his suspicions about what was happening at the warehouse.

"Are you sure it was them?" Sheila asked.

"You know I love you, baby, more than anything in the world and I hate that slut Lisa, but I'll never forget her juicy ass!"

Sheila chuckled and said, "You dirty old bastard."

"I'm going to Youngstown next Wednesday and watch for the truck. I'll probably be there all night."

Sheila's eyes lit up and she pointed a finger in the air. "I have a great idea! I'll go with you, we can both sit up all night and if anybody sees us we can be fooling around a little."

Frank thought this was in fact a good idea. It would be a cover for sitting around in the warehouse district late at night.

"Well, I thought about bringing a girl agent with me," he teased. "But I guess you'll do."

Sheila punched Frank in his chest as hard as she could. The blow caused him to wince but he didn't let on that it hurt. He wondered why her little fist would cause such pain. He laughed and said. "Maybe we should go practice fooling around."

"Sounds good to me," and they headed for the bedroom.

Frank picked up Sheila at her office on Wednesday afternoon and they headed for a Brown Derby restaurant for dinner. They arrived in Youngstown about 8 PM and drove to the warehouse district. Cruising around, they noticed an Enright truck backing into the dock. They drove past and turned around about 500 feet away. They cruised back and saw the driver lock up the truck and head downtown. No one was on the dock and the truck sat silently in its assigned berth. Pedestrian and vehicular traffic had dwindled to almost nothing by the time it was dark and Frank found a vantage point where he parked and watched the truck. Sheila sat next to him quietly, watching for any activity.

"Somebody's coming," she warned Frank and they locked in an embrace.

"This is the best stakeout in the history of law enforcement," Frank said as his hand slipped inside her blouse.

"You're what? 38 years old and already you're the president of the dirty old man club."

"And you love it you hussy, and for your information, I'm 35."

They continued the surveillance until nearly 4 AM. Nobody came near the truck that whole time. "I don't think anything's going to happen tonight," he told a sleepy Sheila, "Maybe we ought to go home."

He started the car and headed once again for the turnpike as Sheila hunkered down in the seat and fell asleep. She didn't hear him say, "I guess most Enright deliveries are legit."

What neither of them saw was the black Chevy parked in an alley across the road and the swarthy looking young man taking down their license number.

CHAPTER VIII

JOINING OF SOULS

Nelson ordered a Manhattan for Dolores and a draught beer for himself. He almost forgot the reason for the date was to discuss the paranormal events. "Tell me more about your relationship with Sheila," she said after taking a sip of her drink.

"I first saw Sheila when I was six years old and although I didn't know why, I wanted to be near her all the time. When we got older and the hormones started acting up I wanted to follow my instincts and she told me she wanted to make love too, but she knew it would ruin our friendship."

"Were you disappointed?" Dolores asked.

"Yes and no. You know where a teenager's brains are. Definitely not in his head. But I loved her so much I didn't want to ruin anything.

"We came close a couple of times but real love won out."

"Most people would call you a wimp, a goody two shoes, but I understand what you're saying. Real love is a powerful force and although it's consummated with the union of two bodies, it also can be consummated by a union of two souls. You and Sheila have joined souls somewhere along the way."

Nelson was fascinated by Dolores' wisdom. "When should sex come into it?" he asked.

"Well, I guess after the wedding, usually."

The salads came first, the crisp lettuce, bright red tomatoes, onion, cucumber all smothered in a chunky blue cheese dressing. Then came the entrees, succulent lobster tails with the little bowl of melted butter, the baked potato mixed with sour cream and butter. The waiter showed the bottle of white wine to Nelson and poured a small amount for him to taste. Nelson approved and the waiter proceeded to pour for Dolores then Nelson.

****

FLASHBACK XI

THE PLOT

The telephone startled Pete in his Yonkers apartment. He rose from his chair where he was watching an episode of the Twilight Zone on his 17 inch Zenith television, and ambled to the instrument in the bedroom. "They should find a way to make these things wireless," he grumbled.

"Hairston?" came the raspy voice over the phone.

"Yes, this is Peter Hairston."

"Do you have someone keeping an eye on your trucks in Youngstown?"

"What are you talking about?"

"There was a car parked near the warehouse last night with a man and woman in it until about 4 AM. Are they your people?"

Pete was becoming annoyed and it showed in his voice. "I don't have people. What do you want?"

"Don't get testy with me, punk, we'll blow your f---ing brains out!"

The hair stood up on Pete's neck at the tone of voice the caller used.

The caller continued, "Those people may have been just getting it on but we ran the license plate and found it belonged to a Frank Richards. Do you know him?"

"Yes, I know him. He became an FBI agent a few years ago."

"FBI? This isn't good. We don't like him snooping

around. I think his credibility needs to be destroyed. Take care of it.." The phone clicked off and only the dial tone could be heard. He hung up the receiver then picked it back up. He dialed Lisa number and after about four rings thought to himself, "she's rolling in the hay with a half dozen people."

"Hello," came her contralto voice, dripping with bitter sweet honey.

"Lisa, it's Pete. Are you alone?"

"Yes Petey boy, but you can't come over."

Pete ignored her assumption and said, "I got a call from Youngstown about Frank Richards snooping around the warehouse."

"Do you think the FBI is on to us?"

"I think Frank might be suspicious, he never liked us anyway, but I don't think there's a full investigation underway."

"Then, we have to find a way to get rid of Frank." Lisa emphatically stated.

They talked about different methods of stopping Frank and Sheila including their outright killing. Killing however would make them more credible and would intensify the investigation.

"We need to convince the 'authorities' Frank is owned by the mob." Lisa mused.

"How do we do that?"

"We need to plant a large amount of cash and some dope on him and make sure the Sheriff or the FBI finds out."

"How much cash?"

"I'd guess at least $20,000."

Pete considered taking the money from Enright but Lisa was afraid that might be a little too risky. Then they talked about the mob giving it to them. Again Lisa was unsure. "They told us to take care of it, that means we have to eat the cost."

"Well," Pete protested, "I don't have access to that kind of cash."

"Bullshit," Lisa said disgustedly, "You're just too damn cheap to come off it."

Pete continued to protest saying his money was tied up in property and other investments.

"Oh, shut up. I'm sick of your complaining. I'll put up the cash but you have to pay me back half you cheap ass son of a bitch!"

Lisa now had more than a quarter million dollars deposited in banks throughout New York, New Jersey and Connecticut. It took a few days to withdraw amounts small enough not to arouse curiosity from any one bank.

CHAPTER IX

CUPID'S ARROW

"What have you found out about Frank and Sheila from your research?" Dolores asked.

"Frank is in the Federal Pen in Lewisburg Pennsylvania. I'm going there next week."

Dolores' eyes widened and she showed the exuberance of a teenager who had been asked to homecoming. "Could I go with you? I want to help you get this straightened out."

"That would be great! I'm taking a few days vacation starting Monday."

They finished the dinner and lingered for a while over dessert and coffee. "I really enjoying being out with you, Nelson." Dolores said.

"I hope we can do this again," Nelson replied then added, "You want to go someplace else now?"

"There's a club in Yonkers called Maxie's. I think Dave Mills is playing there. Do you like jazz?

I'd sit through a Chinese opera with you, he thought but said, "Yeah. I like jazz. Let's go."

They left the restaurant about 10:15 and drove across the Bronx to Yonkers. They found a quiet table near the rear of the room, sat back to sip Manhattans and listen to the mellow tones of the trumpet. After a few minutes she reached across the table and held his hand.

"Thanks for this evening," she whispered.

"I should be thanking you. When I read the account of Frank and Sheila's accident I was really upset. Being with you is making me change my life. I've been a selfish jackass for years but this evening made me realize there are many things that need to be done and Sheila is telling me to get off my ass."

"How has being with me make you see the light?"

"Because you are so wise, so intelligent, so lovely. I want to see you again, date you again and I need to get off my lazy butt and do something about my life."

"It's not a good idea for co-workers to date."

Nelson felt a sadness overtake him until she added, "But that's not going to be a problem."

"What do you mean?"

"I graduated from Hunter College and will soon be entering the banking world. I'm resigning from the post office at the end of this month."

"I often wondered why a classy, intelligent lady like you was wasting away in the post office."

"I had to pay for Hunter College didn't I."

They left Maxie's about one o'clock and walked to the car. After holding the door and helping her into the passenger seat, he walked around to his side. He noticed she slid across to unlock his door instead of reaching across and she stayed in the middle of the seat. Nelson was seated and started the car and he sort of tingled when he felt her body pressed close to him. She rested her head on his shoulder and he could smell the perfume in her hair. He thought, "Can you fall in love on the first date?"

They arrived at her apartment house and Nelson could find no parking spot any place.

"Would you like to come up?" she asked knowing the parking situation made that virtually impossible.

Of course I'd like to come up, he told himself, I'd like to spend all of tonight with you and tomorrow and next week and forever. But he said, "I don't know where I can park."

She agreed the parking situation made the invitation simply a matter of politeness but she was very pleased to be with him. She turned her face to him and their lips touched, then were pressed tightly together. She opened her mouth slightly but did not touch his tongue with hers. Her lips were soft and sweet.

"Call me tomorrow," she whispered and slipped out of his embrace. Nelson exited the car and walked around to her side, opening the door and offering his hand to help her out.

She took his hand and when she was standing they kissed again and she said, "Thanks."

****

FLASHBACK XII

PETE'S GREED

Pete was driving across the Pennsylvania Turnpike in his Caddy with $20,000 cash hidden in the trunk. He also had ten kilos of pot hidden in the front seat. He was grumbling about the ten thousand dollars he had to pay Lisa when the thought hit him. I don't need to plant 20g's on Frank or ten kilos. $8,000 should be plenty. I can pay that bitch back with her own money and make a couple grand for myself. I can even sell some pot on my own. He chuckled. This trip should be worth three or four thousand to me. He checked in to a Holiday Inn in Painesville, Ohio, a city about 30 miles east of Cleveland.

"Where can I rent a car?" he asked the clerk.

The clerk answered with a question. "Why do you want to rent a car, you have a car."

Pete glared at the desk clerk and repeated, "Where can I rent a car?"

Peering over his glasses, the clerk quietly said, "There's a Hertz about two blocks down that way."

Pete drove into Cleveland with his rented dark blue Plymouth. He had secured a city map at the Hertz place and traced a route to Cleveland's southeast side where the Richards' resided. He found the street and cruised along looking for the address. He spied it on his left and noted the garage door was open. There was no car in the garage at this time but Pete wasn't surprised. It was only three in the afternoon and Frank was probably at work. This wasn't New York so there most likely was available parking in downtown Cleveland. It was February and although the streets were clean, there was considerable snow on the lawns and backyards.

He returned to his motel in Painesville and when it was dark, he retrieved the box containing two hundred $100.00 bills. He took out eighty bills and returned 120 to the hiding place. He had ten one kilo packets of marijuana in his front seat. He removed five and concealed the remaining five to be sold without anyone else's knowledge.

He drove back to Frank's street the following morning at 4 AM. It wasn't likely the Richards would leave for work that early. He parked a few doors away but was able to keep an eye on the garage-which was still opened. It was quite cold and Pete was more uncomfortable than he had been in a long time. Nevertheless it was necessary to find out when the Richards left the house and if both were out during the day.

At 7:25 AM Frank and Sheila both came out of the house by the side door, walked to the garage and entered the car. The engine started and a puff of bluish white vapor enveloped the rear of the vehicle. It backed down the driveway, turned towards the place where Pete was waiting, and drove past without seeing him since he had slipped down in the seat.

In his mirror, Pete could see the car come to the intersection and turn left. The vapor obediently followed behind. He started his engine and set the heater on high. He drove for about a half hour then retraced his tracks and returned to Frank's house an hour later. By this time the local children had left for school and the working adults had left for their jobs. Pete had purchased an official looking cap and a clip board. He parked in front of Frank's house, exited the car and walked up the driveway, clip board in hand and official hat perched on his head. He rang the doorbell at the side entrance, waited a few moments than pretended to mark something on his clip board. When no one answered, he walked to the garage. He had the box with $8000 and five k's of pot under his arm. He inspected the side of the garage the front and the track upon which the garage door rode. If anyone is watching me they'll think I'm some kind of building inspector.

He entered the garage, found a shelf with oil cans, paint cans and other sundry junk. He placed the box amidst the clutter then retreated to his car. He drove back to Painesville, returned his rental car and checked out of the motel. He then began his 500 mile journey back to New York.

He stopped at the first rest plaza on the Ohio Turnpike and went straight to the telephone booth. The female voice came from the ear piece, "Cuyahoga County Sheriff."

CHAPTER X

SUNDAY DINNER

Nelson was up around noon on Sunday morning. The house was empty and quiet, the Spivey family having gone to church. Nelson usually fixed lunch for the family for when they returned. It was nothing fancy, just some sandwiches because Vicky prepared a roast something for Sunday dinner. He heard the car drive up and the doors slam as the family came home. The front door opened and Linda burst in and stood before him hands on hips. "Uncle Nelson, do you like your girlfriend more than me?"

"What girlfriend?"

"Mommy told me you were going out last night with your new girlfriend."

"Nah, I don't like her more than you. Can I bring her home to meet you some day?"

"Ask Mommy. I'm not the boss of here. What kind of sandwich did you make for us?

"For you a fat juicy sandwich of weeds and monkey ears."

"Eeeeeeeeyucky!" This had been the ritual with Linda for as long as she was able to understand the joke.

Walter said, "Hey Nelson! How did my jacket enjoy the evening?"

"I spent ten bucks on a new tie for this date and you know what she said? 'Love your jacket.'"

They all laughed and sat down to the *weed and monkey ear* sandwiches. Actually it was bologna on a roll and some iced tea.

"How was church?"

Vicky answered for all, "Very nice, the choir was really good wasn't it?"

Walter nodded.

"How about your date?" Vicky asked

"Great, we had a terrific dinner out on City Island then went to a club in Yonkers. David Mills was playing there. I have to call her soon, she wants to go with me to Pennsylvania when I go to see Frank."

They finished their lunch sat around the table and chatted for a few minutes. Vicky was glad Nelson found someone that might be able to take Sheila's place. He never had a lasting relationship with anyone because no one could compare with Sheila.

Walter said he was going to change clothes then go watch the ball game. Linda already had left, changed into her play clothes and was outside enjoying the late spring weather.

Vicky was getting ready to start Sunday dinner.

Nelson went to the telephone and dialed Dolores' number. His heart skipped a few dozen beats when he heard her say hello.

"Good afternoon to the most beautiful woman in the world."

"Who is this?" she asked. Then she giggled, "I know it's you Nelson."

They talked about the previous evening and how much they both enjoyed being with each other. Vicky motioned to Nelson and said, "Maybe she'd like to come to dinner today."

"My sister wants to know if you like to have dinner with us today if you're free."

"I would love to sit down with a family for Sunday dinner but I don't want to impose."

"I know we've only had one date and it may be a little early to bring you home to 'Mother' but we have known each other for quite some time."

"Well…" Dolores hesitated but it was obvious she would

like a family dinner and she really wanted to be near Nelson again.

"Those squealing brakes you hear are mine. Seriously, I'll pick you up in about an hour if that's OK."

Dolores agreed and 17 minutes later Nelson was shaved showered and dressed and backing his car out of the driveway.

She was waiting in front of her building with a bakery box in her hands. She wore a pretty pink dress and white shoes. Nelson wondered where the bakery was when he saw her some 45 minutes after he left home. Once in the car she moved close to him and kissed his lips. She stayed close to him for the trip back to the Bronx.

They were driving north on the Bronx River Parkway when Nelson asked," Are you still interested in going to see Frank?"

"Oh yes, definitely. I really want to help you clear this matter up."

There was the magnificent aroma of well seasoned roast beef wafting through the house as Nelson and Dolores entered. Linda ran up to them and said. "Hi Uncle Nelson's girlfriend."

"Hi sweetie," Dolores answered. She reached for Victoria's extended hand as Vicky said, "Hi, I'm Victoria, I'm so glad to meet you."

Dolores handed Vicky the cake and exchanged pleasantries with Walter while Linda took her hand and led her to the living room. Vicky disappeared into the kitchen then returned with a pitcher of lemonade and four glasses.

"Maybe you'd like something with a little more zing to it." Walter offered.

"No, no, this is fine, thank you."

They chatted for a while then Victoria excused herself and disappeared into the kitchen again. There were the sounds of pots and pans being moved around, mixers running and the other usual noises, not unpleasant, coming from a typical Bronx kitchen on a Sunday afternoon. Eventually Victoria reappeared with the announcement, "Dinner's ready."

They finished the meal and the desert when Walter said, "That was a great dinner. Shall we retire to the study for brandy and cigars?"

"What Brandy?" Vicky said laughing, "what study? We live in the Bronx not London."

****

FLASHBACK XIII

THE FRAME

The telephone rang in the office of the special agent in charge at the Cleveland FBI office.

"This is Major Ronald Oates of the Cuyahoga County Sheriff's office," came the voice from the other end.

"What can I do for you Major?"

"We've received word that one of your agents may be involved in drug smuggling. Do you have a Frank Richards?"

"Yes, Frank is currently investigating some drug traffic in the Youngstown area."

"Youngstown? Hmmm, it figures,." Major Oates mumbled, "Our sources tell us Frank is doing a lot more than investigating. We are in the process of obtaining a warrant to search his property for illegal drugs. We thought you and your people would like to be in on it. We should be ready to go around eight tomorrow morning."

At the same moment Major Oates was talking to the FBI,

Frank received a call from Joe James in New York.

"Hairston was on the dock again this morning watching the loading of a truck. I don't ask questions anymore but this truck should be leaving here about noon. I thought you'd like to know."

"Yeah, Joe, I'm interested," Frank replied. "You say the truck is leaving at noon? It should get to Youngstown around nine tonight."

Joe who didn't hide his disgust for Pete, muttered, "I hope you get the bastard this time,"

"Thanks a lot Joe, when we get him you'll be the first to know."

Sheila was ready to leave for her office and asked, "Who was that?"

"Joe James," Frank answered, "You ready to go back to Youngstown tonight?"

It was Washington's Birthday therefore Frank was not going to his office. He would be planning the evenings surveillance after he drove Sheila to work. The car had just turned the corner when two Sheriff's vehicles, two Cleveland Police cars and an unmarked sedan with U S Government plates approached from the other direction. Frank and Sheila didn't see the cruisers but the law enforcement people saw Frank. One of the Sheriff's cruisers began to pursue.

In the meantime, the rest of the task force approached the house and garage. They were satisfied there was no one at home and proceeded to the garage. After about fifteen minutes of searching-for which they had a warrant-one of the deputies exclaimed, "Well, well, well. What have we here?"

Hidden behind an old tire beneath a shelf laden with assorted cans and other junk was a metal box and upon opening it, the police discovered a stack of one hundred dollar bills. Further searching turned up five plastic bags of marijuana.

The federal agent in the unmarked car thought, "Frank

isn't stupid. Why would he leave this stuff in the garage?"

Frank had been driving for about five minutes unaware of the Sheriff's car closing in on him. Suddenly a black Chevrolet, not unlike the one parked near the Youngstown warehouse a few weeks ago, darted out of a side street and clipped the front bumper of Frank's car causing him to lose control. The car skidded across the center line and smashed head on into the pillar supporting the overhead railroad tracks. Sheila's head struck the windshield fracturing her skull. Frank's ribs were broken against the steering wheel. The Chevrolet which had no license plates, sped from the accident scene. The deputy sheriff pulled up about thirty seconds later and radioed for an ambulance.

Sheila was pronounced dead at the hospital and Frank was admitted to intensive care in critical condition.

The story went out that Frank was running from the police and no mention was made of the Chevrolet.

CHAPTER X

REVISITED

It was a delightful Sunday afternoon for all. Linda was a little darling and not precociously trying to join in on adult conversation. She continued to call Dolores "Uncle Nelson's girlfriend" until Victoria said, "Her name is Miss Lake."

Walter and Nelson were watching the Yankees playing their usual Sunday doubleheader while Dolores helped Vicky clean up. Finally Vicky asked, "Has Nelson told you about his dreams?"

"I'm not too sure they are dreams. I do believe there is something after death and souls go from one plane to another. Sometimes, the departed can't escape this plane because there is some unfinished business."

Vicky responded, "I never gave much thought to spirits and things although I do believe in heaven and hell. But if there is a God-and I believe there is-there's no reason why spirits cannot exist."

Gradually the conversation moved away from ghosts to the relationship Nelson had with Frank and Sheila.

"Sheila was a wonderful person," Vicky said, "She and Nelson would have died for each other if needed. Her husband Frank was a great guy also. I don't believe the stories about his corruption."

"What about this Pete and Lisa?" Dolores asked.

"I didn't know them very well but from what Nelson says, they aren't very nice people.

I really think they're involved in framing Frank."

"Did he tell you I'm going with him to see Frank?"

"Yes, he did and that's good. From what Nelson tells me you're going to be a great help to him."

The kitchen having been cleaned and straightened up the

two women went into the living room.

"Hah!" Walter shouted, "Your great Mickey Mantle just struck out…again!"

"If I had known you were a Giant fan, I never would have let you marry my sister," Nelson responded, "I'm glad they moved out to California, the turkeys."

Walter, Nelson and Mark, Walter's brother-in-law, would get together on Sundays to argue about the merits of the Yankees, Dodgers and Giants when the three teams were in New York. But since the Dodgers and Giants had moved to California, they were losing their New York identity and becoming just some other teams.

Dolores sat next to Nelson. "I think I've about worn out my welcome, Nelson, so maybe we should get going."

"You stay," Walter answered, "Nelson wears out his welcome every year when the baseball season starts."

They all laughed as Dolores gathered her belongings and asked if she could tell Linda goodnight.

Linda came down the stairs and took Dolores hand. "It was very nice meeting you Miss Lake." Then she whispered, "I still want to call you Uncle Nelson's girlfriend."

"I'd like that." Dolores whispered back.

After the thanks and the invitation to return, and hugs were given all around, Nelson and Dolores entered the Ford. They drove west on 233rd Street and entered the ramp leading to The Bronx River Parkway. Suddenly a light appeared coming from Woodlawn Cemetery. Dolores was perfectly still, frozen in time. Sheila appeared before Nelson.

"She's a good woman Nelson, and she will help you to help Frank and me." Sheila clearly said. "Frank should not be in jail, Lisa should be in jail. She killed Pete you know."

Then Sheila was gone. The light faded out, Dolores began to breathe and move again and the car continued along the ramp to the parkway.

"Did you see that?" Nelson inquired.

"See what?" Dolores' answer was a question.

"Sheila. Sheila just told me you would help me clear up this situation."

"When did this happen?" Dolores looked puzzled and Nelson realized she was unaware that time had stopped for a few moments.

"I just had an encounter with Sheila. I guess I'm the only one who can see her."

"I don't doubt you, Nelson. I only wish I could be gifted."

They continued driving on the Bronx River Parkway in silence.

The car turned on to East 80th Street. They both spied the parking space only two doors from Dolores' building at the same time. "Quick, park there." Dolores said

Once he was parked, Dolores laughingly said, "Would you like to come up for a minute?"

Nelson chuckled back "We had to get the space first, then comes the amenities. I would like to come up."

****

FLASHBACK XIV

GURGLE AND SPURT

Frank was seriously injured in the crash and taken to the hospital, He was placed under arrest and a police guard stationed at his room. The evidence uncovered at his house was sufficient for the federal prosecutor to bring charges. He was also charged with unlawful flight although Frank never knew he was being pursued. When he had recovered somewhat, he had the opportunity to enter a plea. Naturally he said, "Not guilty!"

He wasn't fired by the FBI at least until he was convicted but he was suspended without pay pending the outcome of his trial. But regardless of the final verdict, his FBI career was ended.

Of course, Frank didn't even think about his situation or his career. He was totally devastated by the loss of Sheila.

Pete and Lisa followed the shipment as usual. They registered at a Holiday Inn outside Youngstown and awaited contact from the mob. Pete had given Lisa her $10,000 a few days ago and had sold his five bags of pot for $2,500. Pete answered the ringing telephone and after a few words hung up and said to Lisa, "Let's go. They're ready,"

The unloading and reloading went well and the attaché case was turned over with the index finger to the hat to Lisa. When they returned to the room they dumped the cash on the bed again and Pete asked, "You want to make out on top of the money again?"

Lisa's sex drive was at a low point this night and she said, "Maybe in the morning. Lets just put this back in the suitcase for now."

Lisa awoke about five in the morning and still had no desire for sex. This didn't happen often but it did happen. She opened the suitcase and looked at the money again. It made her smile. She glanced over at Pete who was making rasping sounds from his wide open mouth. "Damn, he's an ugly son of a bitch."

She showered, put on her underwear and began counting the money. By seven o'clock she had several neat stacks of hundred dollar bills which tallied to $168,400. She threw on her slacks and sweater and stepped out of the room, heading for the coffee shop. She noticed a newspaper headline which read;

Dirty FBI Agent Injured in Car Crash
Woman Passenger Killed

The story read;

Acting on a tip, Sheriff Deputies, Cleveland Police and Federal agents raided the house of a fellow agent and found a box containing more than $6,500 and two one kilo bags of marijuana. Frank Richards, the agent, attempted to flee with a sheriff's cruiser in hot pursuit. Richard's car spun out of control on Superior Avenue and smashed head on into a pillar. The woman in the car with him was instantly killed.

Richards was taken to St. Luke's hospital in serious condition.

Lisa stared wide eyed at the story. "That bastard! That son of a bitch! He paid me back with my own f---ing money." Although she was seething on the inside, she was able to maintain her composure and walked towards the kitchen. A young lady approached and said, "Can I help you?"

"Um…Yes, I wanted to get some coffee to take back to my room."

The waitress disappeared into the kitchen and Lisa, rapidly looking around spied a carving knife laying on a counter. She was able to steal the knife unobserved and when the coffee came she sweetly said, "Thank you so much."

Concealing the knife in the newspaper, she returned to her room to find Pete still sleeping. He lay on his side, his face towards the wall. She undressed and slipped naked, into the bed with him. She placed her hand on his genitals slowly stroking him. Pete awakened smiling and turned towards her. The last thing he saw was her evil unblinking eyes as she sliced his throat from ear to ear. The only sound was a gurgle in his throat and that of spurting blood.

She had removed all her clothes not for sexual reasons but so that no blood would be all over them. She returned to the shower, scrubbed herself thoroughly, and began putting her clothes back on. The bed was soaked with Pete's blood and there was spatter all over but Lisa didn't care. She was clean and no one knew who she was. Then she thought, "They knew Pete checked in with his 'wife'. I'll have to account for that."

Taking the newspaper, she cut out the words;

WE...HAVE...THE...WOMAN...WILL...CALL...YOU.

She placed the words carefully on the dresser top, then stuffed all the cash into her handbag and coat pockets and quietly slipped out of the motel. She had taken the keys from Pete and took his Cadillac to a shopping center about a mile away. After parking among several other cars thereby losing the car in the crowd, she walked about a half mile to a car rental agency where she rented a 1958 Dodge Coronet. She asked the clerk for a map and would he trace a route to St. Louis. Leaning over the counter with quite a bit of cleavage showing convinced the agent it would be a decent gesture to accommodate the lady. She was able to show identification and use a credit card issued to Lisa Porter because she was registered at the hotel as Mrs. Rudolph Forfilio.

CHAPTER XI

FEDERAL PENITENIARY

Nelson helped Dolores out of the car and they walked hand in hand to her apartment building. The Security guard in the lobby nodded and said, "Evening Miss Lake."

She answered with a smile and a nod. They walked to the elevator and once inside Nelson put his arms around her and drew her close. She willingly and eagerly accepted his kiss, her mouth slightly open and their tongues touching. When they elevator slowed, they moved apart and stood quietly facing the door which opened on an empty corridor. They smiled at each other and commenced the short walk to her apartment.

"She's a keeper Nelson." Victoria told Nelson when he sat at the breakfast table the following morning. "She seems so nice and intelligent too. Linda's been asking when is she coming back."

"Soon I hope," Nelson replied, "I haven't felt this way about anyone other than Sheila."

Victoria was a very discreet person. She was curious but she did not ask Nelson what time he came home, and Nelson wasn't volunteering anything. "We had an encounter last night," Nelson told Vicky, "Sheila appeared to me but Dolores couldn't see her."

"What did she say?"

"She said Dolores and I together can help set things right. She said Lisa killed Pete."

"I kind of suspected that she had." Vicky said.

Nelson agreed. "There was no evidence that she had anything to do with it. Pete was in Ohio but nobody knows where Lisa was, but who else would want Pete dead?"

Nelson requested and was granted a weeks vacation which he planned to use for his visit with Frank and some investigating. He called Dolores, chatted a while then made arrangements for the trip to Pennsylvania.

He met her at her apartment at 8:00 AM the following morning. She was waiting at the doorway as the Ford nosed up and double parked. Dolores motioned to him to not get out and walked to the car. "Good morning sweetie," she said and they kissed for a little longer than they should have. The Ballantine Beer truck stopped behind them and the driver was sentimental enough to wait fifteen seconds before he hollered out in his best New York accent, "Hey, waddayadoon? Move it!"

Dolores began to giggle as Nelson put the car in gear and they drove off.

"Hey what were we *doon*? How you *doon*?"

Nelson answered, "No, how YOU *doon*."

She was wearing a black sleeveless turtleneck top and black slacks. Her makeup consisted of lipstick and a little blush on her cheeks. Nelson thought to himself, "She's so beautiful. I'm more in love than I was yesterday."

They crossed the George Washington Bridge and headed for the New Jersey Turnpike. About an hour later they crossed the Delaware River Gap and entered the Pennsylvania Turnpike. They stopped at the first rest area in Pennsylvania and settled in for a leisurely breakfast.

"I went to the library yesterday after we talked," Dolores told Nelson, "and studied some newspapers from 1958. The money and pot found in Frank's garage was what convicted him but his fingerprints were not found on the metal box, even though they found his prints on everything else in the garage."

"Well, of course, it was his garage."

"But I doubt if he expected the cash to be discovered so why would he wipe fingerprints from the box? The big question is, why did he hide the money in the garage?"

After they finished the eggs and bacon and were enjoying a final cup of coffee and a cigarette, Nelson said, "They found Pete with his throat cut and blood all over the place.

They didn't know who he was until they ran his license plates a few days later. There was an item in the paper on page 35 about a murder in a motel near Youngstown, Ohio. It said a man who was registered as Rudolph Forfilio was found dead in his room. There was no sign of Mrs. Forfilio who had checked in with him. The police suspect she was kidnapped."

"Rudolph Forfilio?" Dolores asked. "Where did they get that name?"

"It had to be Lisa's idea. Anyway, the murder in Youngstown wasn't big news. The mob is pretty much well entrenched in that area and these things happen quite often there."

They left the restaurant and were back on the turnpike, speeding to Lewisburg. Arriving at the prison just before three in the afternoon, Nelson and Dolores passed through the security area and were ushered into the visitors section. After a few minutes, Frank came through a metal door accompanied by a uniformed guard. He sat behind the glass barrier and picked up the phone.

"Nelson, old man, thanks for coming."

"Frank, this is Dolores Lake, a friend of mine. She is very much interested in justice."

Dolores smiled and Frank smiled back. "I'm very pleased to meet you. You're truly a beautiful woman."

Frank had been in prison for less than a year having been convicted in the summer of 1959. His sentence was for five years which his attorney said was reasonable under the circumstances. "My attorney was an idiot," Frank explained, "He never even questioned as to why I would hide cash and contraband in my garage and if there were fingerprints all over everything else in the garage, why were there were none on the cash box?"

"Why were you running from the sheriff?" Nelson asked.

"I wasn't running. I didn't even know a sheriff's car was following me. The newspapers assumed I was running and wrote it up that way. They called Sheila 'a woman passenger'.

She was Sheila Parks Richards and she was my wife! She didn't need to die and so help me that witch Lisa is going to pay!"

Franks eyes were misty but the angry look and the hatred showing in his face masked any tears that may have formed. Nelson was also angry and filled with hatred because he loved Sheila as least as much as Frank and he also felt she did not need to die.

"This may sound crazy to you, Frank" Nelson finally said, "but I've been visited by Sheila's spirit."

Nelson went on telling of the encounters on the subway and the subway stations and how time seemed to stop when they met. Frank looked at Nelson in a strange manner but shrugged. "I don't know what to think anymore."

****

FLASHBACK XV

FLIGHT TO AVOID

The maid's scream could be heard throughout the entire first floor of the motel. The desk clerk was horrified when he entered the room and saw that Pete was nearly decapitated. The bed was soaked in blood which had dripped onto the floor forming a crimson pool.

A crowd had begun to assemble near the room but the clerk, aware of police procedures closed the door and posted one of his maintenance people to keep the ghouls out.

The police arrived within minutes of the call and secured

the area. "What's this guy's name?" the supervising policeman asked.

"He's registered as Rudolph Forfilio from Buffalo New York." To account for his New York license plates, Pete listed Buffalo as his home. The detectives came and after looking at the registration card, asked the clerk, "What happened to his wife?"

The clerk had completely forgotten about the wife and before he could answer another detective called out, "Hey Bill, come look at this."

The local newspaper was crumpled on the floor with portions cut out. Placed on the dresser was the message about the kidnapped woman. "Who the hell was this Forfilio dude that he was killed and his wife kidnapped?" Bill wondered.

The crime scene unit arrived and performed their duties while Bill decided to further investigate Rudolph Forfilio. The message on the dresser said that the kidnappers would call but not who or when. They instructed the desk clerk to alert them as soon as a call came in. They also made sure the police operator was ready for the call.

The Buffalo police were asked about Forfilio but they knew of no one by that name. A check of the telephone books and city directories also turned up no Rudolph Forfilio.

No telephone call for ransom ever came that day and Bill began to suspect the woman who registered with the victim was in fact the killer. But no one had seen her except the morning waitress and she saw her without makeup and hair up in rollers.

The police began going through Pete's things and discovered a driver's license issued in New York City to Peter Hairston. They also found the registration for a 1957 Cadillac. Bill walked back and forth through the motel parking lot but there was no sign of a Cadillac with New York plates. He said to his partner, "I don't think the woman was kidnapped, I think she's the one who wasted him and took off in the caddy."

Bill returned to the motel manager and asked if anyone had seen Mrs. Forfilio. Eventually a waitress said, "There was a lady who came for coffee early this morning but I don't know who she was."

"What did she look like?" Bill asked.

The waitress described Lisa's five foot seven frame. "She had a pair of boobs anyone of us would have died for."

Lisa drove the dodge to Detroit where she checked into a motel as Lily Brennan. She paid for the room in advance with cash thereby eliminating the need for identification.

The following morning she needed to shop. She had come to Youngstown with only one change of clothes and she had no idea when she would be returning to New York. She had more than $160,000 cash with her so she wouldn't need to withdraw any money from her several accounts for quite a while. She stayed in Detroit for about a week then turned in her rented car. She went to the railroad terminal and bought a ticket to Chicago.

Registering in one of Chicago's finer hotels as Joann Kessenger, she checked the society pages and discovered the more elite places to be seen. She was very beautiful and charming and soon had established herself as one of the jet set. Whenever she was asked about her background she managed to change the subject or she simply smiled and gave no answer.

Of course she slept with several of the men she met and occasionally enjoyed a threesome with another girl. She even had a totally lesbian night with a beautiful model.

Bill, the Youngstown detective was notified that the Cadillac had been found. They checked it thoroughly for signs of blood or anything that might help solve the mystery of Pete's murder. Under the front seat, caught up in a spring was a slip of paper with the name Lisa written on it and the numbers 6520574. Bill filed this away for future reference.

He contacted the Yonkers, New York police for information on Peter Hairston and found out he had no record but the Yonkers policeman added, "we had a tip that he was involved in smuggling drugs."

"Do you know who the tipster was? We would like to talk to him."

"He didn't give us his name but he said he was the dock foreman at some factory in the Bronx."

Bill Evans received permission from his chief and decided to travel to New York City to further his investigation. He arrived at La Guardia three days after the murder, rented a car and drove to Yonkers.

CHAPTER XII

SHEILA'S TWO LOVES

"You said you usually were in or near Woodlawn Cemetery when you spoke with Sheila," Frank said to Nelson. "Funny thing, I've been dreaming about that cemetery pretty often lately."

"Is Sheila buried in Woodlawn?" Dolores inquired.

"She isn't buried any where," Frank replied, "She wanted to be cremated and I followed her wishes."

Dolores thought for a few seconds then said, "There must be some significance to Woodlawn Cemetery. So far nobody has come up with any ideas."

Nelson spoke up, "Woodlawn cemetery had a special meaning to Sheila and me."

They were all silent for a while then Nelson spoke, "Apparently, Sheila wants Frank and me to work together to straighten this out. Pete was killed just after your accident and we all know Lisa did it. The trouble is, no one knows where Lisa is."

Frank added, "No one has connected Pete's killing and my problems. We know Lisa killed him because Sheila told you, but we sure can't take that to the police."

"Why would Lisa kill Pete?" Dolores wondered out loud.

"It probably had something to do with money. Her favorite things in life were money and sex in that order," Frank said.

"Dolores," Nelson suddenly blurted out, "Do you want to go with me to Youngstown? Maybe we can pick up a trail and find the wicked witch."

Dolores agreed readily and since visiting time was just about over, Nelson told Frank, "We'll go straight to Ohio and stop here on our way back. We're going to get you out of here and were going to let Sheila find peace."

When they were back on the Turnpike heading for Ohio, Dolores asked Nelson if he thought Frank believed him about Sheila. "Frank is a practical man but I think he wants to believe. Maybe if I see Sheila again she'll give me something to convince Frank we actually talk. Do you believe me?"

"Of course my darling."

****

FLASHBACK XVI

YONKERS

Bill Evans arrived at police headquarters in Yonkers. and found the policeman he had spoken to on the telephone. Detective Tom Novak of the Yonkers police department was a rather portly middle aged man with a pleasant round face. He accepted Bill's extended hand as Bill introduced himself. Tom said, "I'm just about to go off duty. How about we go around the corner for a cold one?"

"Sounds good to me." Bill answered and they walked a block or so to a tavern frequented by the off duty police-at least, they were supposed to be off duty. When the waitress brought the two Ballantines to the booth Bill and Tom had found, Tom asked, "What's the situation with this Hairston thing?"

"Hairston registered at a Youngstown motel with a women as Mr. & Mrs. Rudolph Forfilio of Buffalo, New York." Bill began.

"Where the hell did they get a name like that?"

"It took some creativity." Bill went on to explain how they found out his correct name and address. "That's when we contacted you folks."

Tom spoke next, "We found out he was the chief finance officer at a factory in the north Bronx. We talked to the owner, a Mr. Enright, who told us he was checking on the warehouses in Pittsburgh and Youngstown."

"You said you got a tip from a dock foreman." Bill said, "Have you spoken with him yet?"

"We planned to go out there this week. When he called he didn't identify himself or his company so we didn't know who to look for. He didn't even tell us where Hairston worked, only that he lived in Yonkers. We watched his apartment for a while but never saw anything suspicious, other than this fantastically built babe that visited once in awhile."

The waitress brought them two more beers and nodded toward a gentleman at the bar. Tom recognized one of the detectives from his precinct and acknowledged the treat with a salute. "We can go to Enright's tomorrow morning if you like."

"That sounds like a good idea," Bill responded, "Can you steer me to a decent motel?"

Tom suggested a place and they made arrangements to meet the following morning.

At nine o'clock in the morning, an unmarked but official looking police car pulled into the motel parking lot. Bill was ready, waiting in the lobby with a cardboard cup of coffee in his hand. "You want some coffee before we go?" he asked.

Tom declined and they began the trip across the Bronx to Enright Industries. They stopped at the 47th Precinct station house to let the New York City police in on the investigation. "There was a murder in Youngstown Ohio," Tom explained to the Precinct commander, "involving a Yonkers resident who worked at a Bronx factory. I don't know who has jurisdiction but if we all go out there everybody is covered."

They entered the main office and identified themselves.

Mr. Enright ushered them into his office and told his secretary to get Joe James. The Youngstown murder was not a national story so Enright was unaware Pete was dead. "He traveled to Pennsylvania and Ohio about once a month to ensure the shipments were proper so when he hadn't shown up here for a few days it wasn't unusual." Enright continued, "What is odd is that his secretary hasn't shown up for about a week. We don't know where she is." Then in a hushed voice he added, "She's a bit of a wild one you know, sleeps around and such."

"What's her name?" asked Tom.

"Lisa Porter," Enright replied.

Bill looked up suddenly at the sound of her name and remembered a piece of paper that was found in Pete's car. He took out his notebook and leafed through it until he found the paper that read, *Lisa---6520574.*

Bill then spoke up, "I think Lisa is the person we need to find. I wonder what this number means."

"You think something happened to Lisa?" Mr. Enright asked.

"We think she killed Peter." Bill answered.

Enright gasped. "Peter was killed and you think Lisa did it?"

At that moment Joe James came in and heard Enright say that Peter was killed. After introductions Joe told of the times Pete would come out on the dock and was nasty if anyone asked him why he was there. "I'm pretty sure he was up to no good, but I don't know if it was something he should have been killed for."

Tom was looking at the slip of paper. "I think this number is a telephone number."

Using their authority as law enforcement personnel, they discovered the number was in fact the telephone number assigned to Lisa Porter of Riverdale, New York. Further investigations with the Yonkers and New York City police revealed Lisa had no record. They went to Lisa's apartment in Riverdale, an upscale section of the Bronx, and spoke with the building manager. Lisa, it seems, is gone for several days at a time, on a few occasions as much as two weeks. "The last time I saw her," the manager explained, "was two days before Washington's Birthday."

"Do you think we could have a look around?" Bill asked.

The manager hesitated saying that Lisa was kind of funny about anyone in her apartment.

"She threw a fit when maintenance went to check her radiators last October."

Bill promised not to touch anything and after a few hems and haws, the manager finally let him in. "If she finds out I let you in, you better have a job for me out in Akron or where ever the hell you come from."

The apartment was clean and neat. There were no dishes in the sink or the drainer. All the trash cans and bins were empty, the bed was made and all closet doors were closed. It was like looking at a model suite. Then Bill noticed what appeared to be a bank book on the night stand. He took a pencil from his pocket and opened the book being very careful not to actually touch it. Suddenly he cried out, "Holy cow! Hey Tom, come take a look at this."

"Whoa!" Tom exclaimed, "she's doing all right for a secretary."

The bank book, issued by the Third National Bank of Hartford showed a recent withdrawal of $3,000.00 and a balance of more than $87,000.00. Bill was convinced now that the missing Mrs. Forfilio was none other than Lisa Porter and she was the person that murdered Peter Hairston.

CHAPTER XIII

CHICAGO

Nelson and Dolores nosed the car into a motel parking lot about nine in the evening. "Shall I ask for adjoining rooms?" Nelson was not going to take anything for granted and would respect any wishes Dolores might have.

"That won't be necessary," she said with her head bent and her eyes looking upward at Nelson. They registered as Mr. and Mrs. Nelson Whitman, and Nelson thought that maybe someday that would be a correct registration. It was still a little early in their relationship but Nelson felt certain he wanted to be married to Dolores and he would sooner or later-preferably sooner-pop the question.

They had no luggage so they went to the room, freshened up a bit and went to the dining room. After dinner they returned to the room which had only one double bed. Nelson couldn't think of a single thing to say and Dolores said, I'm going to take a shower. She disappeared into the bathroom and Nelson listened to running water and Dolores humming. When she came out of the bathroom, she was wrapped in a towel. She went to the bed, turned down the spread and let the towel drop. She slipped her nude body beneath the covers and said to Nelson, "I don't have any pajamas."

Nelson was not aware of his open mouth until she said, "Close your mouth honey and get ready for bed."

Nelson went into the bathroom and noticed her panties and bra drying on the towel rack. He removed his shirt and trousers but got into the shower in his underpants. May as well wash these while I wash me, he mused. He came out of the bathroom naked and quickly slipped into bed. She looked at him and smiled, then they were locked in each other's arms with flesh pressed against flesh.

Dolores awakened first the following morning. She

laughed to herself when she noticed Nelson's shorts resting between her panties and bra on the towel rack. She sang quietly as she prepared for the day and indeed seemed to glow with happiness. She had the same thought Nelson had the previous night. Maybe someday we will be registering legitimately as Mr. and Mrs. Whitman. It was a pleasant thought.

She wakened Nelson and after he had dressed, they went for breakfast. After the meal they lit up cigarettes and dawdled over the final cup of coffee. "These cigarettes are going to be the death of us," Dolores observed.

"Maybe so but it will be a better way to go than how Pete went."

They left the restaurant hand in hand and after she was settled in the car and Nelson had started the engine, he leaned towards her and said, "I love you."

Dolores reached up and kissed his lips and said, "Me too."

They found the Youngstown police headquarters and Detective Bill Evans who was glad to consult with them. He had continued his quest for Lisa as best he could but like any police department, there were too many cases and too few detectives.

"After I returned to Ohio, I canvassed the area around the crime scene and found a place that had rented a car to Lisa Porter," Bill continued, "The clerk remembered her boobs, excuse me Miss, while he traced a route to St. Louis for her, but the car was turned in in Detroit."

"Was there a trail in Detroit?" Dolores asked.

"We found witnesses that remember seeing her shopping in some of the better stores. She bought a whole lot of stuff and paid cash for everything. We assumed she came to Ohio for just a day or two but after the murder, she was staying away from her usual places and she had plenty of cash to live on.

"When she hadn't returned to New York in a month, and since she was now a murder suspect the police executed a warrant and entered her apartment to search for anything that might shine a light on where she was. They found ten bank books from institutions from New Jersey to Connecticut. The balances totaled over a quarter million dollars. Apparently she had enough cash to live for at least two years because we put a watch on the accounts and they haven't been touched yet."

Nelson spoke up, "Do you think she's in St. Louis? She did ask how to get there and may have just used a round about way."

"We found a picture-she had a bunch of them around the apartment, kinda liked herself, I think-and sent it to St. Louis. They haven't found her yet."

Dolores made an observation, "She came from a big city and probably would want big city life. I bet she's in Chicago or Los Angeles."

Nelson agreed and added, "She liked to hang out with the society page crowd and with a lot of money and her looks I'd bet many pictures were taken." Then he asked Bill, "was she listed as a wanted person?"

"Yes," Bill answered, "we sent her picture to police departments in Detroit, St. Louis, Chicago and some other major cities but we got no hits after about four months. Cases that go cold are sort of pushed to the back"

"Suppose Dolores and I do our own investigating. Is there any objection to that?"

"Don't try to be police," Bill warned. "You can check newspapers and magazines but don't try to make an arrest. Call the local police if you find something."

They thanked Bill for his help and promised to let him know what they discovered. They also received assurance from Bill that he would help them in any way he could.

"If we're going to Chicago we need to get some clothes and supplies," Dolores said.

"Should we go back to New York and prepare for a week or so investigating?"

"Don't you have to go back to work on Monday? If we go back and then have to return we'll lose a whole day."

They decided they would get enough clothes to last until Saturday which was four days away, then return to New York on Sunday. Dolores had already submitted her resignation and was just using up her vacation time. Nelson had accumulated quite a bit of vacation and didn't expect any trouble in getting a request approved for additional vacation days.

They drove to Cleveland and checked into the Hollenden Hotel, then walked to Higbees on Public Square and purchased the clothes and supplies needed for the next four days. They were trying on their new clothes in the hotel room when everything seemed to stop.

A soft light filled the room and Sheila once again stood before them. "I'm so happy that you and Dolores found each other," she said then added, "Nelson, even now I love you and I love Dolores."

Nelson felt a certain peacefulness in Sheila's presence but he also knew something had to be done to free her. Sheila spoke again, "Lisa murdered Peter because he cheated her out of some money. She's a cold hearted evil woman who doesn't want anything to come in the way of her money or sex life. She is in Chicago now using the name Joann Kessenger. You're on your own now in getting her."

With that, Sheila faded away and the drop of water that was suspended in mid air resumed its journey to the sink. Dolores looked at Nelson and said, "You talked with her again didn't you?" Nelson nodded and told her what he was told.

The following morning they checked out of the Hollenden and began the journey to Chicago. They both contacted their respective banks in New York and had sufficient cash wired to them. After registering again as Mr. and Mrs. Whitman at a downtown hotel, they formulated a plan to find Miss Kessenger-AKA, Lisa Porter.

"I like the way that Mr. and Mrs. Whitman looks. It would be nice if we could do that all the time," Nelson told Dolores.

"Nelson Whitman! Are you proposing to me?"

Nelson began to stammer and stutter, "N- n-no, I mean-yes, I mean-I don't know!"

Dolores began to laugh, "I didn't mean to put you on the spot, sweetheart, you don't have to say anything else. But for your information, I probably would have said yes."

Nelson had regained his composure. "I know it's too early to propose, and I want to do it properly but, yes, I do want to be married to you."

They fell into each others arms and Nelson kissed her face and her forehead and her ears then her lips. "I really love you Dolores, more than anything in this world."

"And I love you," she replied, "but lets take care of the business at hand first."

The first thing to do was to get newspapers from March 1958 to the present and peruse the society pages for anything that might refer to Joanne Kessenger. They went to the public library and Nelson procured the micro-film for the even months and Dolores for the odd. They began to search page by page and after about two hours Nelson was ready for lunch. Dolores suddenly spoke. "I think I found something."

The newspaper was dated January 23, 1959, and the headline read:

Patrons of the Arts Hold Winter Ball

A photo of the society crowd included in the caption the

names of prominent Chicagoans and one Joanne Kessenger late of New York. Her hair was cut short and was a dark color, probably brown. But the cleavage could not be mistaken by anyone that knew her. This was Lisa Porter.

"That's her!" Nelson excitedly exclaimed which brought a few shushes from the other library patrons. He smiled sheepishly and apologized, then whispered, "I'd know those boobs anywhere. I wish I could see her butt."

Dolores gave Nelson an odd look until he explained, "I hate this bitch, she was responsible in some way for what happened to Sheila. But her ass was one of a kind ever since she was in the eighth grade. Anyone who knew her knew that butt."

"O K, O K, lets figure out how to find Miss great ass." Dolores said, surprising Nelson.

Nelson placed a telephone call to the Youngstown, Ohio police and asked for Detective Evans.

"This is Bill Evans," came the voice over the phone, "what can I do for you?"

"Bill, this is Nelson Whitman. We found Lisa Porter. Is she still wanted?"

"She's wanted for questioning. I'll contact the Chicago police but we have to prove she is Lisa Porter. I'm guessing she's going by a different name."

"She calls herself Joanne Kessenger now, but when she rented the car in Ohio, she used her real name," Nelson said.

"Yes, that's right," Bill answered, "we were looking for Forfolo or something like that. We can't get her out of Chicago but we could get her in a lineup and I can bring the clerk from the rental agency out there. How can I contact you?"

CHAPTER XIV

"WE GOT HER, MAN"

Lisa had established herself in Chicago and was confident Lisa Porter was completely gone, at least until she was needed. She had spent about $75,000 of the cash she took from Ohio leaving her with over $90,000 which would last about a year even while she lived the jet set life. By the end of 1960 the murder of Peter Hairston would be such a cold unsolved case people will have forgotten about Lisa and she could begin withdrawing cash from her east coast accounts.

She had found a luxury apartment, purchased a Buick acquired a driver's license, had telephone service and opened a bank account, all under the name Joanne Kessenger.

Bill Evans spoke with his counterpart in Chicago and explained the situation. "If you can get a fingerprint, we can find out if she is Lisa. I was going to bring the car rental agent out to identify her but if you get the print we can get her in a lineup here."

During the war, companies that held government contracts had to have all employees fingerprinted. Enright Industries was no different. When Lisa murdered Pete, she didn't even think about fingerprints because there wasn't going to be any more Lisa Porter. The Youngstown police found fingerprints belonging to her but they already suspected she was the killer. They just couldn't find her.

One of the jet set crowd in Chicago was a prominent politician who had many friends in the police department. He also had slept with Lisa and that's all they did-sleep. It seems he had a bit of a problem raising the flag, so to speak. Lisa laughed at him and called him limpy from then on. He was of course quite angry with her but after hearing that the police wanted to get her fingerprints, he was glad to cooperate.

He called her and asked her to have a cocktail with him one evening. "I might have an opportunity for you to make some money," he lied.

Lisa still loved the sound of opportunities to increase her wealth and agreed to meet. After ordering drinks, Harold, the politician, said, "I'm sorry I had a problem that night and I wish you wouldn't call me insulting names in public."

Lisa, AKA Joanne, answered, "OK, I won't do it any more," and she smiled to herself.

The waiter came over and took their order. He fumbled for his pencil and pad, dropped the pencil, apologized, picked the pencil back up and scribbled down the drinks. It was difficult to keep his eyes off her barely concealed bosoms.

"Are you okay?" Lisa asked.

"Yes ma'am, I'm sorry, I'm a little nervous."

This was the first and probably the only time a detective sergeant on the Chicago police force would serve drinks to a gorgeous brunette with fantastic cleavage and a big shot politician.

"Pay attention to your trays and quit staring at my chest," Lisa admonished him in her-*I'm a wealthy socialite and you are a lowlife waiter*-voice, "because you won't be staring at anything for a while if you spill those drinks on us."

Harold began explaining the money making scheme. It was a sort of real estate venture, not illegal but not very moral. Lisa was interested and after having the scheme explained, Harold said she would have to invest some cash.

"How much cash?" she asked.

"About $50,000."

"What makes you think I can raise that kind of money?"

"You appeared here about a year and a half ago from nowhere tossing money around like confetti. You never explained where your money came from and I don't care. I'm guessing you amassed a tidy sum that IRS is unaware of."

Harold signaled the waiter by showing two fingers and pointing to their table. The waiter returned shortly and carefully placed the glasses before them, smiling sheepishly at Joanne AKA Lisa. He carefully picked up the empty glasses and when he reached the bar, he put her glass in a plastic bag, discarded his apron and headed for the door. His waiter career was over before he collected a single tip.

The fingerprint was sent to the FBI laboratory in Washington and after a few days, the report came to Bill Evans in Youngstown verifying the fingerprint matched that of Lisa Porter, employed by Enright Industries of The Bronx, New York City.

Nelson and Dolores returned to New York after they were told that Joanne Kessenger and Lisa Porter were one and the same. They stopped off in Lewisburg Pa. to see Frank and give him the good news. While they spoke, time stopped as it had done at the hotel in Cleveland. Sheila stood among the three, although only Nelson could see her, with a background that appeared to be Woodlawn Cemetery. "Nelson, you are wonderful!" the spirit of Sheila exclaimed. "Tell Dolores how wonderful she is and ask her to marry you as soon as you can. Tell Frank I love him so much and that I'm preparing a place for him.

Sheila faded away and the guard who had been in the "ah" portion of a sneeze, resumed with "choo."

Lisa AKA Joanne was mulling over the proposition from Harold. If it was legit, she could make enough so she wouldn't have to touch her New York money for an additional year. The longer she waited, the less likely she would be connected with Pete's murder. She was unaware that members of the police department were approaching her apartment door at this very moment.

She was startled by the rap at her door. Peering through the peephole she saw a large silver badge with the words *Chicago Police Department*. "Miss Kessenger? Detective Tobin, Chicago PD. We would like to talk with you."

"What about?" Lisa asked.

"Please open the door ma'am, we rather not yell."

Lisa was hesitant and wondered what they wanted. They couldn't be asking about Pete's murder. How would they connect Joanne to that? She opened the door to a large rather handsome man in a brown sports jacket and dark brown slacks. He doffed his porkpie hat and said, "Miss Kessenger, do you know a Lisa Porter?"

Lisa's heart jumped for an instant but she was able to recover and answer, "No, should I?'

This tall good looking guy stirred the perpetually burning embers in her loins to flame.

Her dressing gown opened enough to reveal a shapely leg and her hand went to the cleavage that she bared when she looked through the peephole.

Detective Tobin coolly ignored the display and said, "That's odd. One would think two people with the same fingerprints would know each other."

Lisa's sexiness disappeared. She closed her robe and lost her smile. She glanced around appearing to seek an escape route. But there was no chance. A female police officer was with them and Tobin allowed Lisa to dress with the officer standing by. He handcuffed her and led her away saying, "You have the right to remain silent…"

Nelson's phone rang about eleven o'clock that night. "Mr. Whitman? This is Bill Evans of the Youngstown police. We got her, man, Lisa Porter is in a Chicago jail as we speak."

Nelson immediately called Dolores who was ecstatic. Victoria and Walter had retired but Nelson thought they wouldn't mind be awakened for this kind of news. "They got her! The wicked witch is about to have a house fall on her."

CHAPTER XV

A MARRIAGE MADE IN HEAVEN

Lisa was extradited to Ohio and charged with murder. She was identified by the car rental agent, the hotel manager and a desk clerk from a Detroit hotel. She was held without bail in the Mahoning County jail awaiting trial. In an attempt to avoid execution and perhaps receive a sentence that allowed eventual parole, Lisa began to talk. She told them she and Pete had contacted the mob and began the dope smuggling operation. She exonerated Enright and any of his employees who were unwilling and unknowing participants in the scheme. She explained how they framed Frank Richards and even admitted to the maiming of the unnamed lover whom she had blinded.

Nelson went to Dolores' apartment early in the morning following the news from Bill.

She was running towards him as he stepped off the elevator and leapt into his arms. He carried her back to the apartment kissing and squeezing her the whole way.

"We've got to see Frank again and let him know," Nelson said.

They traveled to Lewisburg again the day Frank was released. Meeting him as he exited the prison, he told them, "The FBI is reinstating me, but I'm not going back to work."

"Why not?" Nelson asked.

"For a couple of reasons. First, no matter how long I stay in law enforcement, nobody more evil than Lisa Porter will be captured. Secondly, I have serious lung cancer and the doctors give me only six months to live."

Dolores and Nelson both gasped at the same time. Dolores eyes filled with tears and she sobbed audibly.

Nelson was in shock

"Don't worry about it," Frank said, "this is the best news I could ever have."

Nelson nodded to Frank understanding what he meant.

"Sheila was my only reason for living. But I don't think I could commit suicide. That's the cowards way out. When Nelson mentioned the fooling around practice Sheila and I spoke of, I knew he really was talking to her. We know there is an afterlife so death isn't the worst thing that could happen. Remember when Sheila told Nelson she was preparing a place for me? She knew I'd be with her again.

"I have one request of you guys. Sheila was cremated because that's what she wanted. I was always a little afraid of fire so I'd rather not be burned up. Maybe you could see to it that I am buried in Woodlawn."

Suddenly it became clear to Nelson. The grass on the shoes, the dampness, the earthy odor, Sheila wanted from the beginning to let Nelson know he wasn't dreaming and that Woodlawn would be the connection that would bind them together, forever.

Lisa's trial began in January, 1961, three days after John F. Kennedy's famous, "Ask not what America can do for you, ask what you can do for America."

A jury was selected and given instructions. Opening statements were made by both sides and testimony began. The police presented the fingerprint evidence, the connection with the mob, the statements given to the County Prosecutor and the witnesses testimony.

The defense had no choice but to try for acquittal on the grounds of insanity.

For the first time in more than twenty years, Lisa's breasts were totally covered. She was instructed not to wear any tight sweaters or blouses. Her skirt was mid calf length and it de-emphasized the gorgeous bottom her friends knew so well.

The trial lasted about four weeks at which time the judge told the jury they had four possible verdicts, guilty of murder, guilty of manslaughter, not guilty or not guilty for reasons of insanity. On February 23, 1961 one day after the third anniversary of the death of Sheila Parks Richards-and it would have been exactly three years if February 22 wasn't a holiday-the jury arrived at a verdict.

****

FLASHBACK XVII

FRANK AND SHEILA, TOGETHER AGAIN

Frank was released and exonerated in July, 1960. The FBI paid him for the years he was in prison and accepted his resignation. He didn't tell them he had only six months to live, but left as a hero with a going away party including gifts and proclamations. He decided to return to New York and found an apartment in the Pelham Bay area of the Bronx. Nelson and Dolores as well as Victoria and her family visited him often. Joe James came by a few times once with Mickey the truck driver.

By October the illness showed. Frank had lost about fifty pounds and needed constant nursing care. He was able to afford a private nurse thereby avoiding the nursing home or hospice. Two days before Thanksgiving, 1960, Nelson was leaving work heading for the subway at 34th Street. He had been promoted to foreman in September which made Dolores very happy. As he descended the stairway to the platform everything went dark, then brightened and he once again was standing among the tombstones in Woodlawn Cemetery. Sheila was approaching with a bright smile on her face. "Go to Dolores as soon as you can. I want you two together the next time I see you." Sheila faded away and Nelson continued his descent.

Dolores had begun her career with the bank and was seeing Nelson and his family quite often. Walter told Nelson, "This girl is great. You better get ready for the old ball and chain!" Then he turned to Victoria whose eyebrow was raised a touch, and said, "The old ball and chain is the best thing for a man."

The first thing that Wednesday morning, Nelson called Dolores and told her he was coming to her apartment. "I have something important to tell you."

"I'll be here."

Nelson found a cab on White Plains Avenue and directed the driver to East 80th Street. Parking the day before Thanksgiving was ridiculous in Manhattan. He arrived about noon and was greeted with the delicious kiss he came to know so well. The coffee Dolores had begun brewing was dripping into the carafe when the drops hung suspended, the cuckoo clock stopped with the bird halfway out of the little door and the pigeon that had been flying past the window was now motionless.

Sheila approached through a mist smiling. This time Dolores could see and hear her. She said, "I have someone I want you to see."

Frank then appeared, robust and healthy as he was the day they married and spoke to them, "Your phone is going to ring in a minute, Dolores, I think you know what the message will be. Don't cry for me guys, I'm with my Sheila forever and ever."

Then Sheila spoke to Dolores, "I won't see you anymore but I will be watching over you. I love you both so much."

Nelson and Dolores were startled by the ringing telephone as the real world came back into focus.

"Dolores," came Victoria's voice through the instrument, "I just got a call from Frank's nurse. Frank passed away quietly this morning."

"We knew it was coming but it's always a shock when it actually happens." Dolores said to Victoria, "Nelson and I will be there in a little while."

As he requested, Frank was buried the Monday after Thanksgiving in Woodlawn Cemetery. In addition to Nelson, Dolores, Walter and Victoria, the agent in charge of the Cleveland FBI office as well as the local agents were in attendance along with several World War II veterans, Joe James and a distant cousin from Westport Connecticut, the only known relative Frank had, who was presented with the folded American flag that had draped his casket.

Dolores and Nelson spent Christmas Eve together having a quiet dinner in her apartment. When she got up to get the beautifully wrapped gift she had bought for him, he retrieved the gift from his pocket. She took the box, unwrapped it carefully and opened to a caret and a half diamond set in platinum.

"I love you so very much, my sweetest Dolores, I can't imagine myself not living with you for the rest of eternity. Will you honor me by being my wife?"

"Dear, dear wonderful Nelson Whitman, nothing could make me happier. I'll gladly be your wife."

****

CHAPTER XVI (CONTINUED)

JUSTICE FOR ALL

The jury filed into the courtroom on an unusually warm late winter afternoon in 1961, their eyes focused on their seats in the jury box

"I don't think her Miss goody twoshoes look is going to work for her." Nelson whispered to his wife to be.

Dolores whispered back, "They say when the jury doesn't look at you, you are doomed."

The prosecution had argued that she knew right from wrong, she couldn't be considered legally insane, and with the elaborate plan and method of disappearing, Lisa knew exactly what she was doing. This was the biggest argument in the deliberation room.

When the twelve were seated, and all the principals were in place, the judge asked, "Mr. Foreman, have you reached a verdict?"

"We have your honor."

The foreman handed a folded paper to the Clerk of Courts who in turn handed it to the judge. The Judge read the verdict and handed the paper back to the clerk. "Please read the verdict."

"We the jury being duly sworn find the defendant, Lisa Porter…"

Dolores held Nelson's arm so tightly he started to lose feeling in it as the clerk continued,

"…GUILTY OF MURDER IN THE FIRST DEGREE."

Lisa glared at her attorney, then the jury and the judge with that evil look. Nelson half expected to see her eyes turn red and to smell brimstone throughout the court room. She was led away in handcuffs by a deputy sheriff to await sentencing.

Two weeks later she stood again before the same judge in the same court room.

"A jury of your peers has found you guilty of murder. You are therefore sentenced to be electrocuted in the State penitentiary at such time as the Department of Corrections determines."

There were the many appeals and requests for clemency and then the Supreme Court ruling that the death penalty was cruel and unusual punishment. Eventually, Lisa's sentence was reduced to life imprisonment with the possibility of parole in no less than fifty years. By that time, Lisa would be eighty-six years old.

However, Lisa's sentence ended in the summer of 1979 when after an argument with a large fellow inmate, Lisa was found with her skull fractured in several places. No one claimed her body and she was buried in an unmarked grave somewhere in Ohio. At the very moment Lisa's cell mate smashed her head against the iron bars, a man who had been blinded when his eyes were destroyed by a stiletto heel more than twenty years earlier, and who had lain in a coma since, suddenly smiled then expired.

On a warm and humid August morning in 1979, fifty-five year old Nelson Whitman sat at the breakfast table with the daily newspaper and a half finished cup of coffee. A headline on page six caught his eye.

Prisoner Found Dead in Ohio Women's Penitentiary

Marysville, Ohio August 25,1979

Lisa Porter, serving a fifty year to life sentence for murder was found dead in her cell at the women's penitentiary with a fractured skull...

"Dolores," Nelson called, "come look at this!"

Dolores picked up the paper and shook her head. "Somehow this doesn't surprise me. I guess she shook that tail once too often."

Nelson and Dolores Whitman, stood before a tombstone in Woodlawn Cemetery in the summer of 1979, with their sixteen year old daughter, Sheila, who placed a bouquet of flowers on the grave of someone she never met, but knew so well.

The stone read;

Francis William Richards
Beloved Husband of Sheila
December 19, 1922   November 23, 1960

"You can rest now my sweet Sheila, you can rest easy with your beloved."

It was early in the spring of the year 2213 when two young lovers climbed a hill overgrown with brush in an area that once was a part of New York City. The young lady cried, "Ouch!" when she stubbed her toe on a slab of granite. There was some faint engraving on it and the young man, an archaeology major, stated, "This looks like a grave stone like they used back in the twentieth century and earlier."

The stone was taken to the archaeology department at the university where the scientists were able to restore the writing. They were ecstatic because they had discovered the site of the legendary Woodlawn Cemetery.

END PART 1

WOODLAWN CEMETERY

PART 2

CHAPTER I

THE WEDDING PLANS

On New Year's Day, 1961, Walter and Victoria Spivey invited Nelson Whitman and his fiancée, Dolores Lake, to join them, together with Walter's sister and brother-in-law, for a traditional holiday dinner. Marilyn Decker, her husband Mark, and their son Kenneth lived in Englewood New Jersey having abandoned New York City in 1955 for the suburban life. They did however, enjoy driving to the Bronx on special occasions and discussing with Walter and Victoria the advantages of the suburbs over the city.

"Actually, this part of the Bronx is nearly as suburban as Englewood," Walter would argue, "and we have all the advantages of the city."

"Nelson, do you and Dolores plan to live in the city?" Marilyn asked

Dolores answered, "I love this city. I don't think I'd be very happy in some bedroom community. I'd miss shopping on Fifth Avenue, the theaters, Carnegie Hall, the nasty old subway."

"As long as there are taxis in New York, you won't see Dolores on a subway," Nelson added.

This drew a chuckle from everyone. The men drifted into the den to watch the never ending bowl games. The women retired to the living room and began planning Dolores' wedding. Dolores' parents had passed when she was five years old. She was raised in a foster home by people who cared for her in a loving way. She was never adopted because the foster parents needed the income from the welfare agency during those depression years. The only relative she had was a half sister in Texas who was some twenty years older. They had never seen each other but did exchange pictures from time to time and their only contact was by mail. Nevertheless, Victoria insisted the half sister be informed of the wedding and invited to participate in the planning. Dolores had graduated from High School in 1945 and intended to go to college but her foster mom died that year and she stayed to care for her foster dad until he passed in 1953.

"When do you want to have the wedding?" Victoria asked.

"We want to go on a cruise," Dolores answered, "so I think August would be a good time. You need to book these cruises well in advance you know."

In the den, Walter rose to fix a drink. "Anybody want anything?" he asked. Both Mark and Nelson answered affirmatively and as he was pouring the liquor, Walter said, "The wicked witch goes on trial this month doesn't she?"

Nelson replied, "Yes. Bill Evans, the policeman from Youngstown told me it would begin on January 23."

Mark asked who was the wicked witch and Nelson told him the whole story of Lisa, Pete the drug smuggling operation, the framing of Frank and the death of Sheila.

"Man, she was an evil one." Mark mused. "I remember reading about the guy who was found in an alley with his eyes poked out. She admitted to doing that. I think he's still alive but in a coma. "

Walter changed the subject. "So, how are you feeling about this marriage Nelson my man."

"Hey, she is the greatest thing that could ever happen to me. I can't even imagine my life without her. I'm nearly 37 years old and I never could get serious about anybody. I guess no one could measure up to Sheila, but when I had the encounters somehow I knew she would approve."

"Encounters? What does that mean?" Mark asked.

"We'll explain later," Walter answered, then turned to Nelson. "When is the wedding scheduled?"

"We going to book a cruise for late August, Dolores will set a date. You know I want you to be best man, Walt."

"Well, I would be honored."

When Nelson was promoted to foreman he was transferred to the General Post Office at 34th Street and Eighth Avenue. There was a newsstand that specialized in out of town newspapers in Pennsylvania Station and each afternoon before clocking in, Nelson would buy a Youngstown, Ohio Vindicator to check the progress of Lisa's trial. On February 19, the paper reported the case would be presented to the jury the next day. Nelson called Dolores to ask her if she could take a few days off. She agreed and they drove to Youngstown the following morning. Arriving in mid-afternoon, they went directly to the court house where they spied Detective Bill Evans.

"Mr. Whitman! Miss Lake! Good to see you," Bill exclaimed, "What brings you to Ohio?"

"We've been following the trial and read where the jury was going out soon."

"They got their instructions from the judge this afternoon and will start deliberating tomorrow morning. How long will you be staying?"

Bill spied the diamond, that sparkled like the sun on a gently undulating ocean, and asked, "Is that what I think it is?"

"It certainly is,'" Dolores answered, "and you're invited to the wedding."

Nelson then answered the first question. "We can stay until the end of the week. I hope they come back in by then. I really want to be here for the verdict."

"Well, there's nothing else happening today so why don't we get together for dinner tonight,." Bill said.

Nelson and Dolores checked into a motel making sure it wasn't the one where Pete was killed.

The phone in their room rang just as Dolores was putting the finishing touches on her evening makeup. Her large nearly black, almond shaped eyes seemed to glisten, almost as if they were full of tears. She is so gorgeous Nelson kept thinking as he stared at her shiny brown hair swept up from her neck. Dolores could see him in the mirror and smiled. I love this guy so much she thought.

Bill's voice came through the instrument," We're in the lobby now. You guys ready?"

Bill was dressed in a dark blue suit cut in the Ivy League style. A gold colored pin held together the rounded collar of his white shirt, underneath the two inch wide necktie. He looked like a wall street broker rather than a policeman.

"This is my wife, Angela," Bill said as he introduced a pretty blue eyed lady dressed in a simple but elegant black dress. Nelson and Dolores were both surprised to see Bill with this lovely lady. Somehow they never imagined he was married.

"Bill talks about you two all the time," Angela said, "I'm so glad to meet you at last."

The four left the motel and walked to Bill's green and white Buick. He opened the back door and let Nelson and Dolores in. Nelson said, "There are no handles on the doors."

Bill laughed. "This is my car but I use it for police business from time to time."

They drove for about fifteen minutes to an upscale restaurant outside the city limits.

Bill told the maitre'd his name and the four were led to a booth by a window. In the spring and summer the view would have been quite pleasant but this was February in Northeast Ohio and although the temperature was above normal, the patches of snow here and there, like ratty old blankets, were gray and uninviting. The waiter came to the table and took drink orders.

Dolores took out a cigarette and Bill lit it with the silver Zippo Angela had given him last Christmas.

Angela began the conversation with, "So you're here to hear the verdict on that awful woman who killed that man in the motel."

"Yes," Nelson replied, "This will bring final closure to an epic that started back in 1941."

Bill interrupted. "We're not going to talk about the evil witch tonight. O. K.?" Then he said to Angela, "Have you seen the rock on Dolores' finger?"

"Yes, it's beautiful. You two make a great looking couple."

"How long have you two been married?" Dolores asked

"Forever," Bill answered.

Angela poked Bill in the ribs with her elbow and said, "We've been married for fourteen years. He came out of the navy and was so pathetic I had to do something to save him."

They enjoyed a marvelous salad, steaks, baked potatoes, a vegetable medley and New York Cheesecake with the magnificent coffee sold only in restaurants.. After topping everything off with a delicious after dinner drink they decided to retire to the lounge where a combo was playing dance music. At the completion of the tune they were playing, the leader took the microphone and announced they were going to play the latest thing, the twist.

"Oh, come on Nels, lets try it." Dolores said, taking Nelson by the arm.

"I have no idea how to twist!" Nelson protested.

"Just pretend you stepped out of the shower and you're drying your butt!" Dolores demonstrated.

They returned to the table perspiring and panting. "That's the stupidest dance I've ever seen," Nelson exclaimed.

Bill didn't drink any more alcohol for the rest of the evening because he knew he had to drive home. The others, however, did have several more drinks and by one in the morning they were not drunk but light headed and somewhat euphoric. They laughed and giggled like teenagers yet maintained their mature composure. It became obvious this day that these four would become the best of friends for the rest of their lives. They would be visiting each other as the years passed, sometimes in New York, and other times in Ohio. They met at a Pennsylvania resort, about halfway between Youngstown and New York, for a weekend of fun more than once and went on a Caribbean cruise in the 1980's.

CHAPTER II

THE RUG GUY

Bill called Nelson the day the jury at Lisa's trial came in with a verdict. They met at the courthouse and listened intently while the guilty verdict was read. Afterwards, the four met again for lunch and promised to keep in touch.

There is no scenery on the Pennsylvania Turnpike in February only drab brownish gray leafless trees with a tinge of purple. The dead grass and leaves are a yellow ochre matted mass moving in a blur as the car speeds along. Ugly patches of gray snow cling to the sides of tree trunks, ditches and rocks that never get any sun.

Dolores broke the silence that had lasted about a half hour after they began the drive back to New York. "What a nice couple Bill and Angela are."

"Yeah, I think we're going to see a lot of each other in the future," Nelson answered

The subject then changed to the upcoming wedding and more importantly, the honeymoon. "As soon as we get back," Nelson said, "we have to go to a travel agent and book the cruise.

Nelson tried to find some music on the radio but all he found was some farm reports, Pittsburgh news and lots of country sounds. Eventually Dolores dozed off but was suddenly awakened when Nelson yelled, "Did you see that?"

Dolores was startled and sat straight up saying, "What? What's happening?"

"We just passed some guy dumping a rolled up rug into that ravine. That could be a body!"

"You go to too many crime movies." Dolores said as she waved him off with her hand.

"He looked up when we went past but he probably didn't see us, but I saw him."

"Let's just leave it be. We don't need any problems now."

They continued to drive for an hour then pulled into the service plaza for dinner. They sat near a window and could see their car parked under a lamp. Nelson was about to put a forkful of potato in his mouth when he suddenly stopped and leaned closer to the window. He noted a dark figure walking around to the rear of the car obviously looking at the license plate. "There's somebody looking at our car," Nelson whispered to Dolores. "I think it's that guy who dumped the rug."

Dolores peered out the window and said, "I don't know why I'm looking. I have no idea what he looks like."

"Don't look up! Don't look up!" Nelson warned, "He just came in."

The figure entered the restaurant and was ushered to a table by the hostess. He glanced around the room but appeared not to recognize anyone.

"Quit being paranoid Nels," Dolores said, "He couldn't possibly know who we are and if we witnessed anything."

"Yeah, I guess you're right. He was too far away to read our plates when we drove past, and there was no way he could have seen us in the car. But why was he looking at our license plate?"

"Let's get out of here," Dolores offered.

Nelson signaled the waitress for his check, mentally calculated the tip and put cash on the table. He helped Dolores out of the booth and headed for the exit. After settling in the car, he started the engine, moved the shift lever into drive and pointed the nose towards the ramp leading back to the Turnpike. Neither Nelson nor Dolores noticed the mustached face against the restaurant window watching them continue their journey.

They arrived back in new York near midnight and Nelson drove directly to Dolores' east 80th street apartment. "You want to stay the night?" Dolores asked.

"You know I'd love to but we have a parking problem. I'll see you tomorrow."

They kissed and both said, "Love you baby."

Nelson watched as Dolores entered her building and disappeared into the lobby. As he turned left on 2nd Avenue, a dark blue Lincoln with Pennsylvania plates cruised past the building. Nelson continued driving to the Bronx and as he was about to enter the house, he noticed a big car, a Caddy or a Lincoln, drive up the street. It was unusual for any traffic on the street at this hour so he curiously looked up as the car passed him. He didn't notice the Pennsylvania plates. By 1:30 AM he was snug in his bed.

When he came down in the morning, Walter had left for work and Linda was off to school.

"Welcome home brother," Victoria said as she poured him some coffee, "How was the trip?"

"It was a great pleasure seeing that jury come in and pronounce the witch guilty as sin. She'll be sentenced next week and I hope they hang the bitch."

Nelson then talked about Bill and Angela and what a fine couple they are. "I think we're going to be good friends in the future. They're on the invitation list."

Victoria puttered around the kitchen clearing dishes and putting away things when Nelson said, "A strange thing happened while we were driving back."

"Not an 'encounter' I hope."

"No, I don't think that will happen again. Anyway, we noticed, that is, I noticed because Dolores was sleeping, a man dumping what looked like a rolled up rug into a ravine. Later, when we stopped for dinner we saw this figure checking out our license plate then saw him come in the restaurant. I'm pretty sure it was the guy dumping the rug."

"What was in the rug?" Victoria asked

"I don't know, it could have been a body."

"You've been watching too much Alfred Hitchcock!"

"Maybe so. But why was he looking at our plates?"

After helping Victoria with the dishes, Nelson went to his room and called Dolores.

"I thought about the guy in the parking lot yesterday," Dolores told Nelson, "and I think he was checking us out. Maybe he did see our license plate."

"That could be, but what are the chances of his finding us in this city?"

CHAPTER III

THE MURDER

While Nelson and Dolores were twisting away the night at a lounge in Youngstown Ohio, and Bill and Angela Evans were chuckling at Nelson's awkwardness, Willis B. Sharpe of Bradford Pennsylvania placed the lifeless body of his wife on a blood stained carpet. Kathryn Sharpe, age 27, was the daughter of Arthur Kimble, president and CEO of Kimble Manufacturing. The stains on the carpet were from Kathryn's head which had been smashed in with an ax.

Willis rolled up the carpet and carried it with its grizzly cargo to the garage. He folded it in two and stuffed it into the trunk of his Lincoln Town Car. After he returned to the house, he found cleaning supplies, mops and rags and scrubbed all the walls and floors where blood may have spattered. He then gathered all the items including the ax and placed them into a fifty gallon drum which he had taken from the factory site. Pouring a full five gallons of gasoline over the items he fashioned a gasoline soaked fuse from the rags and ignited it. He stepped back as the drum burst into flame with a sudden whooshing sound. He had heard it was very difficult to destroy a human body completely in a fire, therefore he didn't include it with the clothes and other items being burned. He had a plan that would result in the virtual disappearance of the corpse.

By morning the drum contained nothing but ashes and the steel head of an ax. Willis had a pickup truck in which he placed the drum, on its side. He then began driving the back roads while ashes spilled from the drum and were scattered by the wind into the forest. When he came upon a bridge over a relatively deep river, he tossed the ax blade into the water. The bridge was about two miles from the Kimble mansion. Willis drove a short way on the dirt road next to the river, turned the vehicle so it faced the water and without fully stopping he jumped out. The truck plunged into the swollen river and slowly sunk to the bottom. He walked back to his house, and as far as he could tell, was not seen by anyone. He entered his Lincoln, and began the drive south to the Pennsylvania Turnpike.

He had been traveling on the turnpike several months earlier and noticed a ravine in which fallen trees, brush and debris would hide things for years. There were loose stones piled into the ravine and every time there was a heavy rainfall, these stones were rearranged, and usually further buried any object that happened to be among them. Unless someone was specifically looking for something in that spot, it was unlikely anything out of the ordinary would be noticed. It was then that he decided to get rid of his heiress wife and collect on some of those Kimble millions.

It was late in the afternoon on that dreary February day when he found the spot. He pulled off the main road and stepped out of the car. There were a few vehicles on the west bound lanes but nothing at this moment could be seen on the east bound lanes. He went to the trunk, removed the rug and its gory contents and began dragging it to the ravine. As he was about to dump his load over the edge, a light blue Ford sped past. Willis, who was blessed with extraordinary vision, noticed the driver had turned, possibly to look at him and although he couldn't read the numbers, he could see the distinctive yellow and black New York license plates.

Willis returned to his car, started the engine and pulled on to the main road. He decided to get a cup of coffee and something to eat at the next plaza. There weren't many cars in the lot and the light hadn't quite faded yet when he spied a light blue Ford. He walked to the rear and saw the New York Plates. He jotted the numbers down in a small notebook he carried then entered the restaurant. He glanced around as the hostess found him a seat near a window. He could see the Ford from where he sat and watched to see who would leave in it.

A tall, good looking guy and a gorgeous brown haired lady with almost black eyes got up and headed for the exit. When they went to the Ford, Willis pressed his face to the window watching them. They didn't go to the gas pumps so he guessed they had a full tank and would drive straight through to New York. He also guessed that beautiful sophisticated women was from New York City. If he was wrong the odds of them meeting again were less than those for being struck by lightening; but if he was right, it was good to know who might be a threat.

He left half of his coffee and pie, slapped a five dollar bill on the table and left. He was traveling at 75 miles an hour hoping no Barney Fife type of highway patrolman would get antsy about exceeding the 65 MPH limit. There was a good chance he would never see the Ford again but he decided to try to catch up.

Just after entering the New Jersey Turnpike, in spite of the 11 PM darkness, Willis spied what could be a Ford. He eased closer until he was able to read the license plate. "It's them," he said aloud to himself. He continued past them for a few miles, keeping them in view in his mirror, then slowed until the Ford passed him.

It was near midnight when they crossed the George Washington Bridge and although the traffic was considerably lighter than it would be in the daytime, there still enough automobiles on the road to enable him to follow undetected. There was always some traffic in New York.

Willis followed them to East 80th Street, stopped and turned off his lights when he saw the Ford stop. It sat for a few minutes then he saw the beautiful lady get out and walk into the building. The Ford then drove off and turned the corner on Second Avenue. He followed the blue car to the Bronx and noted where he pulled into a driveway on East 231st Street. The good looking guy from the restaurant on the Pennsylvania Turnpike looked up as Willis continued eastward. Having lived in New York for several years, Willis was familiar with this Bronx neighborhood. He made sure he was completely out of Nelson's sight then turned left on Bronxwood Avenue and again on East 233rd Street. He headed west on East 233rd Street--it was too late to try to return to Bradford-so he decided to stay over. He found a motel in Riverdale and turned in for the night.

He would return to Bradford the following day and in a panic, report his wife missing. He awoke at nine o'clock, dressed, and stopped in the restaurant for breakfast. He had carefully hung his clothes last night so except for some stubble on his chin, did not appear disheveled. Besides, in New York, no one noticed anyone else. Before he started his journey back to Pennsylvania, he ran the license plate number and found it belonged to one Nelson Whitman of the Bronx, New York.

CHAPTER IV

WHAT IS IT ABOUT BRADFORD PA?

On a cool but pleasant Saturday in March, Nelson and Dolores walked into a Bronx travel agency and inquired about a Caribbean cruise. They booked a medium priced outside cabin for the week of August 26th to September 2nd. "You'll fly to Miami," the agent told them, "and set sail about midnight. You'll sail all day Sunday and dock at Curacao early Monday morning." The agent continued with the itinerary and the couple accepted the invitation to the pre cruise meeting where the customs of cruising would be explained as well as suggesting the best places to go and things to do.

Returning to East 231st Street house, Nelson picked up the paper while Dolores sat in the kitchen chatting with Victoria. A small article on page 19 read:

Pennsylvania Heiress Still Missing

Bradford Pa March 11,

Pennsylvania State police and the McKeon County Sheriff Department continued their search for missing heiress, Kathryn Kimble-Sharpe...

Somehow, this story meant something to him. Nelson had a strange feeling when he read it but couldn't tell why. It was a feeling he had just before the encounters at Woodlawn Cemetery. "Sheila my sweet, I'd love to see you again," he thought, "but I really don't want any more encounters and I promise to stay off the Woodlawn express!"

Sheila didn't appear but the news story remained clear in Nelson's mind.

Out in the kitchen, Victoria asked Dolores if she had contacted her half sister. "I wrote to her a couple of days ago but haven't received an answer yet," Dolores replied, "I asked her if she would take the place of my mother. She's about 55 now and she never married. I don't know why."

Linda came bounding in and ran straight to Dolores. "Hi Uncle Nelsons girlfriend!" This appellation for Dolores was accepted by everyone now and Linda would call her that at least until Nelson and Dolores were married. Walter came in a few minutes later and Victoria began to prepare dinner. After greeting Dolores with a peck on the cheek he offered Nelson a beer-which was readily accepted-and sat down to watch the news on TV.

"In Bradford Pennsylvania, the State Police and the County Sheriff's Department continued to search for Kathryn Kimble-Sharpe who disappeared two weeks ago. Her husband has offered a five thousand dollar reward to anyone that finds her. Her father, millionaire Arthur Kimble also has offered five thousand dollars."

When he heard the newscaster reading the story, Nelson's hair stood up on his neck and a chill ran through his entire body. Walter noticed Nelson's shudder and asked, "You OK man?"

"Yeah, I'm fine. Its just that this is second time I heard about that Pennsylvania woman's disappearance and got this weird feeling. Is Bradford Pennsylvania anywhere near the Pennsylvania Turnpike?"

"You still thinking about that rug guy?"

"Well, she disappeared around the time we saw the rug guy."

Dolores came into the room and heard Nelson say, "rug guy."

"You still worried about our evil, murderous, body dumper?" she asked.

"I'm not worried about it but I just keep having these odd feelings. Oh well, let's forget about it. We have more important things to think about."

They finished the Saturday supper Victoria had prepared and retired to the living room to watch *Have Gun, Will Travel*. Linda cuddled up close to Dolores pushing Nelson to the side.

"I'm still going to move in with you and your husband when you get married you little bug," Nelson told Linda.

"No you're not! Because I ain't getting married ever!"

"Am not," Victoria corrected.

After *Gunsmoke* ended, Nelson got up and said, "You ready to go home Miss Lake?"

The drive back to Manhattan was uneventful and they luckily found a parking space close to the apartment house. Nelson walked with her into the lobby and on to the elevator. They got off to a corridor as deserted as a schoolroom in late July, and proceeded to her suite. As soon as they were inside he took her in his arms and kissed her very passionately. She responded in kind and within fifteen minutes they were in the shower together.

The sun was fairly high in the sky when Nelson awoke to the aroma of freshly percolated coffee. Dolores was in her robe, her hair rolled up in curlers that looked like frozen orange juice cans. A kind of net like cover was stretched over the cans. She wore no make up and Nelson thought how beautiful she still is. "I love you baby," he blurted out.

"I love you too Nels," she answered. "Would you get the orange juice from the fridge?

A large pitcher of juice was on the top shelf and Nelson dutifully brought it to the table. He noticed several of the concentrate cans neatly stacked in a cardboard box. "These cans make great rollers in case you were wondering," Dolores explained.

They finished breakfast and were relaxing with that final cup of coffee and a cigarette.

"I'm quitting these things soon," Dolores announced, "Have you been reading those reports about cancer and stuff?"

Nelson nodded in agreement but made no commitment. Before he could speak the telephone rang. He heard Dolores squeal, "Margaret! How are you?"

"I got your letter and couldn't wait to give you an answer." Margaret's unfamiliar voice said, "I'd LOVE to be your surrogate mother for your wedding. I'll come to New York around the end of July. Do you think you can put up with me for a month?" This was the first time Dolores actually heard Margaret's voice. All communications had been by mail.

"Not only could I put up with you, I'll put you up! You can stay here with me."

They chatted for a while and after hanging up, Dolores turned to Nelson and said, "That was my sister from Texas. She's coming here for a month and will be a part of the wedding."

"Sounds good. I'm looking forward to meeting her. Did you both have the same father or mother?"

Dolores explained that her father was born in 1879 and was a real cowboy. He was raised in Texas and married a city woman who had come to the Lone Star State as the nineteenth century turned into the twentieth. She wanted to bring some civility and culture to the wide open spaces. Margaret, their only child, was born in 1906 but because there were no modern hospital facilities in those remote regions, her mother died in childbirth. Jacob Lake was devastated and took his baby daughter to New York. He no longer wanted the frontier life, however he spoke glowingly of Texas often enough, that she decided she wanted to go there. Margaret was raised and schooled in New York and although she had no recollection of where she had been born, she decided to move to Texas when she was nineteen.

Jacob remarried and this union was blessed with a beautiful baby girl in 1927 who was named Dolores. In 1932 tragedy struck the family. Jacob Lake and his wife were driving their Pontiac to White Plains New York when they were struck head on by an out of control dump truck. They were both killed instantly and Dolores became a ward of the state.

"So you never actually saw Margaret," Nelson stated

"We usually enclosed pictures in our Christmas cards but no, I've never seen her."

CHAPTER V

THE SEARCH FOR KATHRYN

Willis Sharpe returned to Bradford late in the afternoon after his journey to New York. He checked the area around his house for signs of anything that might be suspicious. He entered the house and examined all the walls, floors, nooks and crannies for blood spatter. He made certain there was no blood or fibers from the cleaning rags in the bathroom or anywhere else. Then he went to the telephone and called his father-in-law.

"Mr. Kimble, is Kathryn there?" Arthur Kimble never liked his daughter's choice for a husband but accepted him for her sake. However, he refused to allow Willis to call him anything but Mister Kimble.

"No, she isn't here. Where were you?"

"I had to go out of town last night and just got back this afternoon. The pickup truck isn't in the garage but her car is." It wasn't unusual for Willis to leave town in the evening and stay away all night. Arthur suspected he was having an affair or making some shady deals but there was never any evidence of such carrying on.

"Have you called the police?" Mr. Kimble asked. He felt uneasy about the fact her car was still there.

"Not yet. I thought she might be at your house. She's done it before when I wasn't home, although she usually left a note."

"I think you better call the police now."

Willis called the sheriff's department and within the hour police and sheriff's cars were stopped this way and that all over his driveway and the street in front of the house, their red white and blue light bars flashing like so many Christmas trees. Officers were probing around the garage, the tool sheds, and the grounds. Detectives were questioning Willis,

Arthur and the housekeeper but no light was shed on the situation. Eventually the State Police and the F B I were called in.

Two weeks passed and there was no ransom demand or any contact with the family.

Willis and Arthur offered $5,000 dollar rewards for any information on Kathryn Kimble-Sharpe.

Throughout the Spring the rivers were swollen from melting snow and considerable rain. But as May turned into June, there had been three weeks without rain and the river levels began to decrease. A teenage boy walking along a dirt road spied what looked like the top of a truck in the middle of the river and notified the authorities. The truck was retrieved and examined thoroughly by local, state and Federal officials. If there had been any evidence in the truck, it was washed away by river water flowing over the vehicle for four months.

Kathryn was now presumed to be dead by Arthur Kimble and his associates but the police believed she had run off. Willis appeared to be totally shattered.

CHAPTER VI

THE WEDDING

As the weeks passed, Victoria and Dolores worked on getting the wedding together. Dolores introduced Margaret to Victoria over the telephone and together they worked out detail after detail. Margaret had a few friends in Texas she wanted to invite who said they'd be happy to travel to New York. Her social circle included some people who owned considerable amounts of Texas oil, and this would be a great opportunity to do some shopping on Fifth Avenue.

Nelson and Dolores did not see each other every night. Nelson, being a junior supervisor still was required to work nights more specifically, the first tour, midnight to 8:30 AM. She had her work with the bank and at the end of the day all she wanted was her hot bath and relaxation. Nelson awoke one spring evening and while waiting for Victoria to finish preparing dinner, sat in front of the television to watch the news. It was the usual thing, a shooting in Brooklyn, a fire in the South Bronx, a bank robbery in Manhattan, a rescue of a trapped animal in Staten Island (not all the news was negative) and then the discovery of a truck in Pennsylvania.

"A sixteen year old boy hiking along a back road near Olean New York discovered a pickup truck in the McKeon river. A trace of the license plate revealed it was the truck belonging to Willis Sharpe of Bradford Pennsylvania. Mr. Sharpe's wife, Kathryn Kimble-Sharpe who is the daughter of millionaire Arthur Kimble, disappeared in February and no sign of her has been found. A reward of ten thousand dollars has been offered for information about her whereabouts but police fear she won't be found. No ransom demand was ever made after her disappearance."

Nelson felt a chill run through his entire body and he

began to tremble and perspire. The feeling only lasted a few seconds but Nelson felt apprehensive. He looked around the room, out the window and back at the television. The same sensation he had when Sheila appeared came over him. A commercial for Budweiser Beer was now being broadcast.

He wondered why any mention of Bradford Pennsylvania caused these feelings. He called to Linda. "Baby, would you bring me the Atlas in your room?"

Linda brought the book and Nelson turned to the map of Pennsylvania. He found Bradford in the north central portion of the state, close to the southern tier of New York State. Why would the mention of some hick town make me feel so uneasy, he wondered.

After dinner he called Dolores. "Hi sweetheart, how you doing tonight?"

They made small talk for a little while then Nelson mentioned the newscast and the feeling he had. "Do you know anything about Bradford?" he asked.

"I have no idea where it is and what it might... wait a minute." Dolores' face lit up although there was no one there to see it. "Do you think this has anything to do with the rug guy?"

"I don't know. Why would that have anything to do with us?"

"Somebody was checking out our car."

"I checked the map and Bradford is 80 or 90 miles from the turnpike. Why would anyone carry a body that far to dump it?"

"How do you know she was killed in Bradford?"

"Are you ready to do a little investigating? We're pretty good at it you know."

"I think maybe we should get this wedding thing over with first."

121

The usual activity preceding a wedding continued through June and into July. There were fittings of the wedding dress, the outfits for the bridesmaids and matron of honor, the decorations, the cake and mailing of the invitations. Nelson purchased silver cuff links for Walter, his best man, and Mark and a fellow postal supervisor, his groomsmen.

On the last Saturday in July, Nelson and Dolores were at Idlewild Airport awaiting TWA Flight 56 from Dallas. On board was a striking five foot three brown eyed bronze skinned woman who appeared at least ten years younger than her 55 years. Margaret Lake chatted amicably with her seat mate as the four engine Constellation began its descent into New York. When the announcement came that the passengers could now disembark, Margaret turned to her new friend and said, "It was so nice traveling with you. I do hope we meet again sometime."

She climbed down the portable stairway that had been pushed up against the aircraft and walked towards the terminal building, her hair blowing in the wind. Modesty demanded she hold her skirt close to her body lest the billowing garment revealed more than what should have been seen in public. As she entered the terminal building, she looked around for her sister whose face she had only seen in a photograph.

Dolores also had only a photograph to go by which she had brought with her. She scanned the faces of the passengers and compared them to her photo. Suddenly Nelson spoke up. "Hey, that lady over there, she looks like you."

Dolores checked her photo and Margaret stared at her. "Dolores?" Margaret inquired.

"Yes, are you Margaret?"

"I certainly am."

They embraced each other and Margaret spoke first. "I'm so glad to finally meet you. You are so beautiful."

"I guess I must be because Nelson said, 'that lady looks like you.'"

Dolores introduced Nelson who was immediately hugged and kissed by his soon to be sister-in-law.

While they drove back to the city, Margaret told Dolores about their father. Dolores remembered very little about him but Margaret was with him for nineteen years. "He was a real cowboy and I think he wanted to go back to Texas but he also blamed Texas for taking away his wife, my mother."

"A real cowboy?" Nelson asked. "you mean with a gun and everything?"

Margaret laughed. "As a matter of fact he did carry a gun when he was out in the wild but it wasn't to see who had the fastest draw. Disputes were settled in courts in spite of what Hollywood says."

As they crossed the 59th Street bridge, Margaret could see the Empire State Building in the distance. "We Texans think everything we have is big but that Empire State Building makes anything in Dallas look like a hut. This is the first time I've actually seen it you know."

When they reached the Manhattan side of the bridge it was only a few minutes to Dolores' apartment--traffic willing. Margaret was a good luck charm because as they approached the apartment house, a car pulled out of the space directly in front of the door.

Nelson pulled right in, helped the ladies from the car and retrieved the luggage. Dolores and Margaret walked ahead chatting away while Nelson struggled along with four suit cases in which Margaret had packed nothing but pure lead, or so it seemed.

"This is a lovely apartment, Dolores, do you and Nelson plan to live here?"

"For a while, my lease will run out in November and

then we'll find *our* place."

Margaret retired to the bathroom to freshen up and Dolores whispered to Nelson, "How do you like her?"

"She's fantastic and is almost as gorgeous as you!" Nelson then changed the subject, "Where do you want to go for dinner tonight?"

"How about that nice restaurant in Yonkers? I hear the food is great."

Margaret reappeared and when they told her the dinner plans she was more than agreeable. "But I don't want you guys to think you have to do special things for me."

Nelson went back to his sister's house, showered, shaved and dressed for dinner. He wore a light sport jacket and an open collar shirt. The restaurant wasn't so strict one needed a tie but they did expect gentlemen to wear jackets and ladies in dresses. Dolores wore a bright yellow sleeveless dress and Margaret was lovely in a lime green outfit. Heads turned when the three were escorted to a booth. The dinner was delightful and the cocktail lounge afterwards included a piano playing crooner.

Margaret insisted Nelson dance with her-not the twist-and when they were on the floor she told him how glad she was to finally meet her sister and to know she was going to marry such a wonderful man.

"Shucks Ma'am," Nelson drawled and Margaret said, "That was the worst Texas accent I ever heard. Don't ever do that again!" They had to return to the table because their laughter made dancing impossible.

The waiter brought three drinks to the table and pointed to a portly gentleman at the bar. Nelson waved to Tom Novak, the policeman who had a small part in the capture of Lisa Porter. He beckoned Tom to come to the table.

"Thanks for the drinks detective, you know my fiancé Dolores and this is her sister Margaret."

"A pleasure ma'am," Tom said with a slight bow.

Nelson smiled to himself, thinking about his attempt at Texas talk but Margaret didn't notice anything since she was used to being called *Ma'am*.

"I understand that case is all cleared up now," Tom said.

"Yeah, the witch is in the joint right now waiting for that electrifying moment."

Margaret looked puzzled and Dolores told her the whole story except the encounters.

"Boy, she was something," Margaret said, then added, "How did you know where to look for her?"

"It's a long story."

Nelson picked up Margaret and Dolores early in the afternoon the following day. Victoria was as usual preparing Sunday dinner for all of them and Linda was anxiously waiting to meet "Uncle Nelson's Girlfriend's Sister". Even Linda knew this title would be rather cumbersome and decided to call her Miss Lake. However Margaret thought that sounded a little too stiff but she didn't think children should call adults by their first names. "How about you call me Aunt Peggy."

Victoria and Margaret hit it off beautifully. It was as if they had known each other forever. While Nelson and Walter drank beer and watched the Yankees on TV, the ladies stayed in the kitchen chatting about everything from Margaret's social life in Dallas to the upcoming wedding. "Please don't misunderstand, I'm not being a name dropper but a few of my friends will be coming to New York for the wedding. They come from big oil money in Texas and want to do some shopping at Saks, Lord and Taylor and such. I hope you don't mind."

"Not at all," Victoria said, "If they're anything like you I think we'll have a ball. Of course, I won't be shopping with them."

"Neither will I," Margaret answered with a chuckle. "They're great friends but I work for my money and I need it."

When August began in 1961, most of the wedding preparations were complete. Friends dropped by Nelson's house and Dolores' apartment with wedding gifts which were all displayed in Linda's room. Linda was more than cooperative in giving up her space. Besides, it was fun sleeping on a cot in the basement. Dolores, who was very organized, kept a little book with the names and addresses of all gift givers with the gift listed. It was Linda's job to keep the book safe. Walter maintained the RSVP's and was able to give the caterers two weeks notice. They checked on the cake and made sure there were no problems with the reception hall. Dolores had a final fitting for her dress and the men assured their tuxedos were ready.

On Monday, August 14, Nelson and Dolores attended the meeting at the travel agency for the people going on the cruise. They would travel as a group but were not obligated to each other. A fairly rotund gentleman with a thick black mustache and the unforgettable name of Sherman Furman was the group leader. Mr. Furman was an employee of the travel agency and had led dozens of groups on Caribbean cruises. He explained the dress codes for dinner including a formal Captains dinner the second night out, the tipping customs, where to get bargains on shore trips and what areas to avoid. "Some of these islands have areas infested by gangs and hoodlums who prey on tourists who stray from the beaten track. The main areas are well patrolled by local police. If you don't want to go to the usual tourist haunts, I suggest you stay on board."

A voice came from the back of the room, "If you have a license, can you carry a gun?"

"I cannot stress enough that guns are strictly forbidden. Even off duty law enforcement personnel should not carry guns. The cruise lines are governed by the rules of the flag they fly under and except for St. Thomas, all the ports are foreign countries and their laws apply."

"Shoot," Nelson whispered to Dolores, "I was going to bring my Tommy gun."

"There's only one gun I want you to bring!"

"Oh, you wild horny old broad you!"

"Hush, Sherman Furman is speaking."

"I wonder if his middle name is Herman? And is he German?"

Dolores covered her mouth to smother the giggle and added, "Does he like Ethel Merman?"

Sherman gave a disapproving glance to the snickering couple but continued, "We sail at midnight Saturday and will be at sea all day Sunday and Monday. Sunday night we will have a section of the lounge reserved for our private party and Monday night will be the Captains Dinner and reception. Thanks for coming and we'll see you on the 26th."

Bill and Angela arrived on the Friday before the wedding. They checked into a Manhattan hotel and called Nelson.

"Glad you could make it," Nelson exclaimed, "How's your accommodations?"

"Couldn't be better. Anything we can do to help?"

"Nah, we've got it under control. The rehearsal is tonight so we'll see you tomorrow."

A bachelor party was proposed but Nelson was not enthused. "I don't need a final fling because all I want is to be married to Dolores. Besides, strippers bore me and drinking is no big deal anymore. I'm 37 years old you know."

Andrew and Frances Whitman, the parents of Nelson and

Victoria lived in Florida but arrived in New York on Saturday morning. Victoria managed to squeeze them into Linda's room for a couple of nights. They would be returning to Florida on Monday. Margaret's friends arrived Friday evening and checked into the Plaza Hotel. They spent Saturday contributing handsomely to the retail stores on Fifth Avenue.

Everything was coming together for the big day The only thing left for Nelson was to get his hair cut and go downtown to see Bill and Angela. Dolores was at the beauty shop for her nails and a spectacular hair do.

Nelson left the barber shop and started to drive downtown. He was on the FDR drive, when the music playing on the radio ended. A voice came on announcing the noon news.

A special segment called unsolved cases was a feature of this particular newscast.

"It's nearly six months since the daughter of millionaire Arthur Kimble disappeared and the local police, the State police and the FBI are no closer to a solution. There has been no contact with the family and no sign of Kathryn Kimble-Sharpe of Bradford Pennsylvania since February 23rd of this year."

A sudden sharp pain seared Nelson's brow and an icy chill went through his body. The sound of an automobile horn shocked him back to reality. "What the hell is this thing with Bradford Pennsylvania?" Nelson asked the empty seat next to him.

When he got to the hotel he met Bill and Angela in the lobby. They went into the restaurant and were seated, awaiting their lunch. "Bill, have you heard about this girl who disappeared in Pennsylvania?"

"You mean the millionaire's daughter? We got a flyer asking us to keep a lookout for her just like most police departments. All our patrol cars carry the picture around but this case is going pretty cold now."

"Whenever I read something about this disappearance or hear something on the radio this feeling goes through me like a lightening bolt. I can't understand why this case would have anything to do with me."

"Didn't you have some kind of supernatural visions in the past?" Bill asked.

"Well, yes but I know it sounds kind of crazy." Nelson was hesitant and a little embarrassed talking about his visions.

"I've never had any visions or experiences with the supernatural but that doesn't mean they don't exist. I have no reason to believe you didn't talk with a ghost. Anyway, what I'm thinking is that someone is trying to contact you about the Bradford case."

Angela spoke up. "Bill was always a practical man who dealt with facts. Everything had a natural explanation. Then the department was stumped on a case and a psychic was called in. The case was solved from the information she gave. From then on, he had an open mind about everything."

The three sat quietly for a minute or so thinking about the situation. Bill broke the silence with, "Well there's a lot more important things happening tomorrow so we better clear our heads now. Ain't that right friend Nelson?"

At about 4 AM on Sunday morning, August 20, 1961 the multitude of stars in the heavens began to wink out, one by one, as a deep red glow appeared on the Eastern horizon. Soon only Venus was visible and the sky was a cobalt blue. Then even Venus disappeared and the sky turned into gold and if the crash of cymbals could be visualized, it would be the sun bursting into view. A single white puffy cloud floated in the eastern sky and as the solar disk rose, that cloud began to dissipate. This promised to be the most glorious day of the entire year.

The guests began arriving in mid afternoon for the four o'clock ceremony. Dolores and the attending ladies arrived at 3:45 PM and performed the finishing touches, fussing with this and fluffing that and flicking away imaginary dust motes. Nelson and his best man, Walter, waited in the wings with the minister while the groomsmen ushered the guests to the pews. Bill and Angela looked at each other puzzled, when asked, "Bride or Groom?"

"We love them both equally," Bill quipped, "maybe we should sit in the aisle."

They chose the bride's side and smiled at the other guests in their immediate vicinity.

An usher escorted Andrew and Frances Whitman to the reserved seats in the front pew. A second usher then escorted Margaret to the front pew on the opposite side of the aisle as the organist played the fanfare that introduced Mendelssohn's Wedding March.

Linda led the procession strewing rose petals along the white satin runner. Kenneth Decker, Victoria's nephew followed with the rings. There was an intentional pause, done for the dramatic effect, then the bridesmaids and groomsmen slowly walked down the aisle, reached the sanctuary and took their places.

Dolores had no escort, no one could take the place of her real father who she never really knew or her foster father who had passed away eight years ago. She was silhouetted against the light streaming in from the open church door. As she moved forward, details began to emerge. The oohs and aahs, and the gasps were audible throughout the church. Nelson had known Dolores for several years and had been engaged to her for the past eight months but today, he was seeing her for the first time. Walter leaned towards him and said, "Close your mouth."

"I never knew there could be anything so beautiful. This must be what heaven looks like," he whispered back. The minister smiled and nodded in agreement.

Her dress was a floor length strapless ball gown with a basque waistline and a cathedral train. It was more ivory in color than pure white. She held a bouquet of white roses in front of her and smiled at the guests on the right and on the left. She puckered her lips and made a little kissing sound at Margaret who was grinning from ear to ear even as her eyes filled with tears.

She took her place next to Nelson who lifted the lacy veil over her head.

"Who gives this woman?" the minister asked.

"I do," answered Margaret as she raised her hand.

The ceremony went off perfectly. An associate of both Nelson and Dolores from the post office sang the wedding song and after the minister gave Nelson permission to kiss the bride, he turned to the congregation and said, "Ladies and Gentlemen, may I present Mr. and Mrs. Nelson Whitman."

Nelson looked out at the people who went out of focus, and saw Sheila and Frank surrounded by a glow, smiling and nodding. Frank gave the thumbs up sign and they disappeared. The entire congregation applauded as the bride and groom marched arm in arm to the wedding recessional thundering on the church organ.

The wedding party entered the waiting Cadillac limousine and proceeded to the photographers studio for the formal wedding pictures. The guests continued on to the reception which was held at the Concourse Plaza Hotel across from the Yankee Stadium on the Grand Concourse in the Bronx.

Virtually, all the guests were assembled in the ballroom. The announcement came over the loud speakers and quieted the sounds of voices, laughter, clinking of glasses and music from the four piece combo. The bridesmaids and groomsmen were introduced, then, Nelson's parents and Margaret Lake as Dolores' surrogate mother.

"The Best Man and the Matron of Honor, Walter and Victoria Spivey." The assemblage applauded politely then broke into an enthusiastic cheer as the announcer said, "Ladies and gentlemen, Mr. and Mrs. Nelson Whitman!"

Nelson and Dolores smiled broadly at the guests and waved with their free arms while they encircled each other's waists with the other. Nelson whispered into Dolores' ear, "I saw Sheila and Frank in the church."

"What?"

"It was just for a second and they showed me their approval."

After the dinner was completed, the obligatory dances were done then the fun dancing-including the twist, which Nelson and Dolores performed admirably as was expected since they had practiced as often as possible. The married couple thanked everyone, kissed and hugged where necessary and excused themselves. They would leave the following morning on the Atlantic Coast line for Miami where they would spend the rest of the week, but tonight, tonight the honeymoon begins.

Nelson and Dolores had slept together before and thought they knew everything about each other. But this was the first time Mr. and Mrs. Whitman slept together and they would learn what true intense love could do for the extraordinary pleasures of their bodies which in turn would bring happiness beyond their dreams.

The door was securely locked and the "Do Not Disturb" sign was hooked to the outside doorknob. "Let me get out of this dress," Dolores announced with a sigh and Nelson helped her unbutton the voluminous garment. He watched her carefully hang the dress in a garment bag and then remove her slip. Clad only in her panties, bra and a garter belt, she began removing her stockings as Nelson became more and more aroused. Dolores had to smile when she looked at his cute buns as he hung his tuxedo in the garment bag while totally naked. He turned around and heard Dolores, now looking at his crotch, say, "Whoa!" She disappeared into the bathroom and after a few seconds the door opened slightly and her underwear was tossed to Nelson.

He heard the water filling the tub, then it was quiet. Nelson was in the tub with Dolores less than a second after he heard, "It's awfully lonesome in here,"

After a long period of lovemaking, Nelson said, "We need to get some sleep."

There were twin beds in the room but of course they planned on using only one but Dolores agreed, they needed some sleep. She left his bed and slipped under the covers of the other one. Nelson got up and went into the bathroom. When he returned he looked at a still awake Dolores in the other bed and decided to slip into it with her. "I thought we were going to sleep," she said with a giggle.

"Yeah, yeah, sleep." Nelson replied as he positioned himself between her legs.

Eventually they both dozed and after a half hour or so, Nelson awoke to see Dolores peacefully sleeping, the covers kicked off and her beautiful buttocks exposed. He moved over to the other bed so she wouldn't be disturbed. He awoke when he heard the toilet flush and looked up to see his beautiful naked wife standing over him. She slipped into the bed with him and moaned audibly as his hand slowly moved over her genitalia.

The following day on the Atlantic Coast Line, two sleepy people dozed in their seats as the streamlined train sped towards Florida.

CHAPTER VII

THE CRUISE

United Airlines Flight 276 arrived at Miami International at 2:10 PM August 25th. On board was the mustached Willis Sharpe and 22 year old dancer, Karen Van Horn. They checked into the Holiday Inn on Collins Avenue in Miami Beach from which they would board the cruise ship, Island Queen, on the following day. Arthur Kimble agreed it might help the grieving Willis if he got away for a while. Of course Arthur was unaware that Willis would be meeting the voluptuous Miss Van Horn at the airport.

Three days after he murdered his wife, Willis drove to Buffalo New York to do the things a single man about to come into a bucketful of money would do. He found a night club where the entertainers and the waitresses were not encumbered by a dress code. In fact as long as the most intimate parts of their bodies were not visible, they were within the law.

Willis signaled a pretty young nearly naked dancer to come to his table for a drink. This was permissible by the club as long as there was no physical contact. A very large man whose collar size would have been a nineteen if he had a neck, stood close by to ensure the club rules were followed.

"You're quite a talented dancer. What's your name?" Willis asked.

"Karen," she answered and thanked him for the compliment and the drink which was 95% orange juice and 5% grenadine but cost the same as a double shot of whiskey.

She told him that they were not allowed to date customers but Willis was a charming man and eventually she whispered she would meet him at another location after she was off.

They spent the night together and Willis promised to call

her in the future. At first it was just part of his line. "One bimbo is as good as another," he told himself, but he really enjoyed the fantastic sex with her and he did call. He had two rules however. She was never to come to Bradford and she was never to call him. As long as Willis was in Bradford or at the plant he moved around like the heartsick widower everyone expected him to be. Even Arthur Kimble would eventually expect him to start dating again but surely not for at least a year. After all, no one knew if Kathryn was dead or alive-except Willis

It was about a three hour drive to Buffalo from Bradford and Willis made the trip two or three times a week. Occasionally he would try to pick up other women but he always returned to Karen. As they lay together after an active period of time, Willis said, "How would you like to spend a week or so on a cruise ship?"

"For real Will?" she screeched.

"Of course for real. I'll book a cruise through the Caribbean as soon as possible."

On Saturday, August 26, Willis and Karen joined hundreds of other vacationers at the pier waiting to board the Island Queen. A steel band played the island songs including the standards, *Yellow Bird and Guantanamero* as well as some of the new Calypso pieces made popular by a young singer named Harry Belafonte. Servers walked among the passengers dispensing hors d'oevers and rum punch. It was after 4:00 P.M. when the announcement came that passengers may now begin boarding. Nelson nudged Dolores and nodded towards the shapely little lady walking with the mustached gentleman. "I wonder if she's the entertainment," he whispered, "she looks like a chorus girl."

The couple passed Nelson and the man's arm lightly brushed his arm. A sudden chill went through Nelson's body. It was the same feeling he always had whenever Bradford Pennsylvania was mentioned. Dolores noticed him shiver and asked, "Are you OK?'

"Huh, oh yeah, I don't know what happened. I'm fine."

After finding their cabin and freshening up, they headed for the lounge to await the dinner call. The group leader, Sherman Furman, explained that on the first night one could sit wherever he wanted in the dining room but after that tables will be assigned for all meals. Dolores sat in a booth with a sixtyish couple from their group, while Nelson went to the bar. The four departed for the dining room when the call was made and were joined by a young couple from Canada. Dinner was delightful and the sextet had a grand time learning about each other. They returned to the lounge after dinner and found Sherman.

"Could we all sit at the same table for dinner?" Dolores asked.

"I guess that could be arranged." Sherman replied.

Just before midnight the ships horn blasted a notice to all of Miami that the Island Queen was about to sail. Julia and Matt, the Canadians and Will and Esther the sixtyish pair joined Dolores and Nelson on deck. They watched the hustle and bustle occurring on the dock which was slowly moving away. After a few minutes they could feel the gentle swaying of the vessel as it headed out of the port and into the open sea.

It was near noon on Sunday when the three couples met near the swimming pool. Dolores wore a white bikini and caused many heads to turn; Julia was in a flowered green and yellow bikini and Esther was in bathing attire suitable to her age. They sunned themselves at the pools edge occasionally dipping their toes in the water. The waiters brought exotic tropical drinks with paper umbrellas on tooth picks and pieces of pineapple impaled on swizzle sticks. Other attendants would move through the crowd with spray bottles filled with cold water. They would ask if one wanted his body cooled down and then would gently spray the sun bather. Music of the islands filled the air mixed with the squeals of children and splashing of water in the pools.

The captain announced they were on a southeast course and would arrive at Curacao at 8 A.M. the following morning. The ship was moving at 18 knots creating a comfortable steady breeze along its length. A canvas awning covered an outdoor bar where the sextet met for a libation. Nelson and Matt ordered cold beers while the ladies sipped delicious Rum punches. Will was content with a ginger ale having developed an ulcer while participating in the rat race. He was now retired and planned on cruising with Esther whenever possible. Matt was a contractor in Windsor Ontario and Julia was a homemaker. They had a four year old and a two year old that Grandma and Grandpa were more than happy to keep for a week or so.

"Isn't that the chorus girl sitting over there?" Nelson asked Dolores, nodding towards the other side of the bar. Karen Van Horn was clad in a lemon yellow very brief bikini that concealed nothing.

"Careful Will," Esther said, "you don't want to make that ulcer act up again."

Julia then said, "Careful Matt, you don't want ME to act up!"

Everybody laughed heartily and returned to their conversation. A mustached man joined Karen and glanced around the bar area. Nelson's eyes met those of Willis for a brief moment but it was as if time stopped. It seemed both parties recognized each other but did not know from where.

Nelson returned to reality when he heard Dolores say, "I guess we better start getting ready for the cocktail party." Julia stifled a giggle and winked at Dolores who began to flush. She smiled back at Julia and began her walk arm in arm with Nelson, back to their cabin.

"You know, this shower is a bit cramped for both of us," Dolores said as they attempted to lather each other up.

"Yeah," Nelson replied, "but it sure is fun."

They managed to put the soap away and move back and forth beneath the cascade of water eventually rinsing away all the suds. Nelson spread out two towels on the bed and they lay there naked. While still soaking wet, they embraced and made love passionately, then, after taking separate showers, prepared for the cocktail party and dinner.

Dolores wore a strapless lemon yellow dress that came halfway between ankles and knees. Nelson wore his black suit with a tuxedo shirt and black bow tie. Sherman Furman had told the men they didn't need to have tuxes as long as they had black or navy blue suits. They attended the cocktail party and passed pleasantries with the others in the group, and after about an hour they were ready for dinner. They entered the dining room and spied Will and Esther already seated. Will who had been on several cruises over the years did have a tuxedo and he looked quite debonair. Esther was very lovely in a floor length beige gown, her shoulders covered by a matching chiffon shawl. Julia found her way to the table and Matt, who seemed to know everyone on the ship came along after shaking hands, waving and greeting as many of the passengers and crew he could. He was not the dress up type but he did wear a dark suit and tie even though he was quite uncomfortable.

"You know, back home he hardly speaks to anyone." Julia offered. She sat next to Dolores and whispered to her, "I had some too!"

Dolores smiled and flushed a little. "Go away," she whispered back and smiled.

The waiters brought the first course to the diners. There was the usual chatter throughout the room, the clinking of dishes, silver and glass, the occasional roar of laughter from one group or another. Music, which no one listened to but everyone heard, played softly in the background.

Karen Van Horn entered wearing a skin tight red silk dress. It was unlikely she wore any underwear because there didn't seem to be any room between the fabric of the dress and her. At least half of her bosoms were visible and although covered, her nipples where easily discernible. Not a few men were brought back to earth by a not so subtle poke in the ribs or kick in the shins. Then Willis Sharpe entered, paused for a moment and looked around the room. The image suddenly changed for Nelson to a Howard Johnson restaurant on the Pennsylvania Turnpike, six months earlier when a mustached man entered and looked around but did not seem to recognize anyone.

"It's him!" Nelson excitedly said to Dolores.

"Who?" She asked puzzled.

"The rug guy!"

"Oh. C'mon Nels. You think he knows us? Do you think he's stalking us?"

"No, I think it's a coincidence but I'm certain that guy with the chorus girl is the rug guy."

They noted where Willis and Karen sat and Nelson frequently looked over at that table. However, he never saw either one of them look back at him. "It isn't likely he recognizes us." Dolores said.

"I suppose you're right. But I can't forget he checked out our license plate."

CHAPTER VIII

THE COCKTAIL LOUNGE

Karen overheard the tall guy with the pretty lady say "…Chorus Girl…" as she and Willis were boarding the ship. She wished she were a part of the entertainment on this boat. "Cruising through the Caribbean all year long, dancing, stripping, what a great life," she thought to herself. He didn't have his hands on any of the Kimble millions yet but he was well off enough to afford a suite above deck. As soon as they were in the suite, Karen removed her clothes and stepped into the shower. Willis joined her a few minutes later, their shower being sufficiently large enough to accommodate two people. They decide to pleasure each other rather than go to dinner and soon after the cigarettes they were both sound asleep.

They awoke in time for breakfast then headed for the pool area. Karen's bathing attire was as brief as it could legally be and she drew stares from all the men and most of the women. She noticed the tall guy looking at her and saying something to the pretty lady in the white bikini. Willis joined her and said, "You'd drop that bathing suit in a second if they allowed you to. You really don't need to because we can see everything you got anyway."

"If they have a topless beach or a nude beach on any of these islands I'm going there."

"I don't give a f-k what you do as long as I keep getting your goodies."

Karen was a little annoyed with that attitude. She loved being naked and showing herself off but she would like to think she meant more to a guy than a roll in the hay. But, he's spending money on me and I'm going to have a great time, she told herself.

They sat at the bar all afternoon, Willis drinking martinis

and Karen very light rum punches. By four o'clock Willis was quite drunk and needed Karen to help him back to their suite. He collapsed on the bed muttering something that sounded like, "the bitch should be rotted away by now…they'll never find her…want the money."

"What? What are you saying, what money?" Karen tried to ask but Willis was now totally unconscious.

Karen removed her useless swim suit and stood in front of her closet selecting a dress for tonight's dinner. The red silk looked pretty good. She showered again and was sitting in front of the mirror clad only in her panties, fixing her hair when she heard Willis stir. He opened one eye then the other, rubbed his head and said, "Oh boy! What the hell is going on?"

"You were kind of loaded Willis, and you passed out. Are you going to get ready for dinner tonight?"

"Yeah, I guess so. Turn on the shower for me will you, all cold."

Karen obeyed as Willis removed his clothes then stepped into the icy cold water.

"Ayieeeee" he screeched but then settled down and let the water rinse away the cobwebs that had grown in his head. When he came out of the shower Karen had donned the red dress and was smoothing it over her curvaceous butt.

"I can see your drawers under that dress baby."

"Oh shoot, I guess I can't wear any panties tonight."

Karen finally was ready to go to the dining room. Her nipples and her bare buttocks fought to free themselves from the confining red silk fabric. "I think you're going to either cause some divorces or have some old biddy get a little tonight," Willis said with a laugh.

She went on ahead and was assigned to a table. She noticed the tall guy and the pretty lady sitting with a young guy who looked very unused to wearing a suit, a cute little lady who probably was a mommy glad to be away from the kids for a week. There was also a very distinguished looking older couple sitting with them. Willis came in and glanced around the room, spied Karen and walked to the table. There were two other couples at the table and the gentlemen found it very difficult to keep from staring at Karen. The women looked at each other raised their eyebrows, tightened their jaws and almost imperceptibly shook their heads. There wasn't much conversation at this table that evening.

Karen was an exhibitionist. She wore clothes that revealed as much of her body as she could and loved to walk in front of windows totally naked. But Willis noticed how uncomfortable many of the passengers were with the men trying to avert their gazes and the women clucking and he really didn't want to call attention to himself. He told Karen he was pretty tired and wanted to return to their rooms. Karen was disappointed but followed him to the stateroom. She thought about slipping out after he fell asleep.

When they got to the room and were preparing for bed she said, "What did you mean when you said you want the money? What money are you talking about?"

"When did I say that?" Willis asked, responding to her question with a question.

"When we came down here after you got drunk at the pool bar."

"What else did I say?"

"It wasn't clear but it sounded like they can't find her or something like that."

Visions raced through Willis' head like a sped up movie film. He was swinging the ax, Kathryn was bleeding as he rolled her up in the rug, the ashes were flying out of the barrel in the truck, the blue Ford with the New York plates sped past on the turnpike, the name Nelson Whitman on the automobile registration list. "I don't know what you're talking about."

142

"I know you're keeping something from me but that's OK," Karen said in a very serious tone, "but don't think I'm stupid. I'm here to have a good time, I love the ship, I love the food and the entertainment and I love showing off my body as much as I can. And oh yes, the sex is terrific.

"I don't want to go to sleep now so I'm changing this dress now, putting on some underwear, and going back to the lounge."

Willis was a little surprised to hear her talk to him that way but he shrugged and told her she could do whatever she wanted. "But I hope you come back here to sleep."

She sat at the bar next to the tall guy who had been with the pretty lady and said, "Hi."

Nelson responded with, "Hello, how are you?" but he seemed a bit aloof. The young guy who looked so uncomfortable in a suit came up to the bar. He had removed his tie and jacket by now and spoke to everyone he passed including Karen.

"You cruise often?" he asked her.

"No, this is my first time."

"Yeah, it's the first time for me and my wife too, eh."

The two men carried back drinks for themselves and the other four sitting in a booth. Karen picked up her drink and walked over. "Could I sit with you guys for a while? I'm here by myself tonight."

Julia scooted over and the seven were a bit crowded but not uncomfortable. She introduced herself. "My name is Karen."

Matt made the introductions, "This is Nelson, his wife Dolores, and this is Will and his beautiful wife Esther."

Esther turned to Will and said, "I think I'll trade you in for Matt's twin brother-if he has one."

They talked and laughed and had a pleasant evening together but only Dolores noticed Nelson seemed to be

143

somewhat troubled."

After dinner the sextet found a booth in the lounge where Dolores and Julia scooted to the rear discussing cosmetics. Matt removed his tie and jacket and Nelson hailed the waitress.

They ordered a round of drinks and chatted about this and that with occasional burst of laughter punctuating the conversations. The lounge began to fill up and Nelson couldn't attract the waitress' attention so he decided to go to the bar himself to get the second round. Matt volunteered to help but it took him at least three times as long to get from point A to point B because he had to stop and talk to everybody.

Nelson was seated at the bar waiting for his order and was mildly startled when he heard, "Hi!"

Nelson turned and saw the chorus girl still dressed in a sexy dress but not quite as revealing as the red silk in the dining room. He looked around to see where the rug guy was but didn't see him. "Hello, how are you?" he said somewhat coolly. He recognized her as the rug guy's girlfriend and felt uneasy in her presence.

Matt came up and after greeting the ship's engineer, sat next to Karen and exchanged pleasantries. He picked up three of the drinks while Nelson took the other three and they headed back to their booth. A few minutes later Karen approached the booth and asked if she could join them. "Sure," Esther said and they all moved to make room.

Karen told them about her life in Buffalo and although somewhat shocked at first they all came to realizing a stripper was a person like anyone else and could be a delightful conversationalist.

"Honey, if I had your boobs, I'd display them all over town!" said Esther which caused Will to choke on his drink. Everybody laughed except Nelson who kept one leery eye on her and the other on the entrance watching for Willis.

Dolores leaned closer to Nelson and whispered, "Lighten up baby, she seems like a really nice girl."

"She's the rug guy's girlfriend and might be feeling us out."

"Oh stop being so paranoid."

At midnight Will announced that it was well past their bedtime and he and Esther would be retiring.

"Don't do anything I wouldn't, eh." Matt called out.

"I wish I could do what you wouldn't," Will muttered but loud enough for all to hear.

The laughter drowned out Esther's response, "Me too."

The five stayed at the table for another hour or so enjoying the music, the laughs, occasional dancing and watching the single fellows trying to figure out which one of these three beauties was unattached. Even Nelson began to warm up to Karen who was in fact a delightful person. She displayed her body not to attract men but because she was proud of it and honestly felt it was her duty to exhibit herself like it is the artist's duty to share his creations. The conversation came around to Willis and how she came to be on the cruise with him

.

"He told me his wife ran off with somebody and he had no idea where she was. After a while he was so lonely he'd drive up to Buffalo for some city life. He came from some hick town in Pennsylvania called Bradford."

Once again time stopped. The twist was being played and the dancers were suspended in grotesque positions. The cymbal over the drummer's bass drum was motionless at a 45 degree angle after being struck an instant earlier. Cigarette smoke stopped on its way out of or into people's mouths. The only movement clearly visible in Nelson's mind was a picture of a man dumping a rug in a ravine.

Then suddenly the sounds of music and people having a

good time returned. The dancers resumed their contortions, the cymbal reverberated, the smoke continued along its various paths. As soon as Karen finished the word Bradford, Dolores looked at Nelson. She noticed the beads of perspiration that had formed on his brow. She put her hand on his arm and asked if he was O K. Nelson didn't answer for a few seconds and Dolores repeated, "You O K Nelson?"

The others hadn't noticed Nelson's distress but when Dolores repeated her question they all stopped talking and looked at the honeymooning couple. "What happened?" Matt asked.

"I'm all right," Nelson answered, "I just got a sudden sharp pain in my head, like a migraine. It's gone now."

It was just about time for the evening to end anyway so Dolores said, "I guess we should call it a night."

Everyone agreed and they said their good nights and headed for their respective staterooms. Nelson lay on his back in the bed his arm bent at the elbow and beneath his head. Dolores was snuggled up under his other arm which encircled her upper body. His eyes were wide open and Dolores could sense his anxiety.

"I'm convinced," he announced to Dolores, "that Karen's boyfriend is the rug guy and that the rug guy dumped his wife's body along the Pennsylvania turnpike."

"Well, I'm coming around to your side. His wife just disappeared? I don't think so,." Dolores said.

"So what happens now?"

"What happens now? What do you think happens now? The great detective team to be known from this day forward as 'The Whitmans' will bring this curmudgeon to justice!"

"What's a curmudgeon?"

"I don't know, I just like the word. Now gimme a kiss."

CHAPTER IX

KAREN VAN HORN

Now that they both accepted the situation and had a plan the tension subsided. They both slept well that night and appeared at breakfast the following morning relaxed and ready for a day of touring Caracas, Venezuela. Two dozen busses lined up at the dock ready to take tourist to visit this South American city. Sherman told his group to remember the number of their bus lest they become lost and spend the rest of their lives in the Amazon jungle. "Only kidding," Sherman said, "if you miss your bus the government will kick you out of the country."

Caracas was a beautiful city, the white buildings untouched by industrial soot. The six stayed together admiring the beautiful parks and plazas, where Nelson spied high in a tree, that crossword favorite, the three toed sloth. They visited the shops and purchased caps, T-shirts, and other interesting souvenirs. The tour included lunch in a huge arena that could accommodate up to 5,000 people with an orchestra playing favorite Latin American tunes. When the band leader called, "Let's Cha, cha, cha!" at least four hundred participants crowded the dance floor.

The tours continued taking them to several interesting points in the city and surrounding area and finally returned them to the ship with just enough time to freshen up and dress for dinner.

As the six sat at their assigned table and sipped their cocktails, Karen and Willis entered. Karen smiled and waved to them while Willis glanced over then continued to his table.

"You're in trouble now, Buster, the Whitmans are watching you." Nelson said aloud but not loud enough for

Karen and Willis to hear.

"What does that mean?" Matt asked.

Nelson started to answer but Dolores interrupted. "Nelson swears that guy is a bank robber and we're going to capture him." Nelson looked at Dolores but decided to go along with her. Some couples were dancing while they awaited their dinner and Nelson said, "Oh, that's our song. Let's dance."

When they were on the floor Dolores asked him since when did they have a "Song."

"Since now," Nelson answered. "Why did you stop me from telling them?"

"They seemed to have liked Karen and so did I, but I'm afraid they might say something to her. If he is the rug guy and I think he is, he'll know we suspect him and might come looking for us. We have to go back and give them some silly reason why you think he's a bank robber."

They returned to the table and Dolores was laughing almost uncontrollably. "Nelson says," Dolores paused for a moment and snickered, "he says, that guy has a thick mustache and no ear lobes and somebody did a study that says that people with those characteristics are usually robbers." She continued laughing. "I asked him where he read about this study and he said, 'Mad Magazine.'" Everybody began laughing and soon the whole discussion was forgotten.

The rest of the cruise was glorious. Karen didn't come down to the lounge alone anymore. She would sit with the six for a few minutes but Willis was not interested in making new friends. He stayed at the bar nursing his drinks. Nelson and Dolores were both happy about this arrangement and the others merely shrugged and said the hell with the crab. Karen had found her nude beach and proudly walked around in the all together. She was a little disappointed because although she drew some stares, they were no more than she would have gotten in a bikini on the regular beach. The crowd that pranced about the beach were no different than those at a regular beach. Nudity was not exciting or shocking to nudists.

The shipped dock at two more islands during the next two days finally stopping at St. Thomas in the Virgin Islands where the ladies went wild shopping at the duty free stores.

They sailed from St. Thomas at 6:00 PM Thursday evening and arrived back at Miami on Saturday afternoon. Matt and Julia gave hugs and kisses all around and promised to keep in touch, then boarded their plane for Toronto. Will and Esther headed for Detroit and Nelson and Dolores boarded Eastern Airlines for Idlewild Airport. Since the cruise was six days after the wedding, they wanted to go to Florida leisurely on the train but they were anxious to return home so they flew back.

They arrived in New York late in the evening, collected their luggage and caught a cab for East 80th Street. The night security man was on duty and greeted them with, "Welcome home Miss Lake...I mean...Mr. and Mrs. Whitman."

"Thanks, Charlie," Dolores said, then asked, "Did my sister get away all right?"

"Oh yes, three billionaire women came by in a limousine and picked her up."

The honeymoon ended and the marriage began at that moment.

CHAPTER X

THE MARRIAGE

When they disembarked from the ship and collected their baggage, Willis and Karen headed for the railroad station. When they left Buffalo a week earlier, they were anxious to get to Florida so they flew down. But they looked forward to as much time together as possible for the return. They would return by train traveling first class to extend this vacation by a day. However, during the cruise they became somewhat bored with each other although Karen was afraid to admit it. They had fantastic sex night after night and the train trip would add several more hours of sex but this was all they had. Willis would either sleep or totally ignore Karen when they were between sexual encounters. She was somewhat angry at his attitude on the ship and how he wouldn't even meet her new friends. As they neared Buffalo they began arguments which increased in intensity and finally he struck her.

"You son of a bitch," she screamed, "you son of a bitch. You're not getting away with this you bastard!"

"Oh shut up slut." he retorted and slapped her with the back of his hand. Blood flowed from the corner of her mouth and she cried audibly.

"I hate you, you f-k," she sobbed and went into the bathroom to tend to her injuries.

They detrained separately, and although most of the other passengers had no idea what went on in their compartment, the conductor noticed Karen's swollen jaw and reddened eyes. He shook his head feeling real pity for this sexy little lady.

Willis got his luggage and tossed hers to the side. He had a car parked at the depot for his trip to Bradford, stowed his bags and began the three hour trip with no concern as to how she got home. Being a practical person, Karen had the foresight to keep a few hundred dollars on her person just in case something like this happened. She hailed a cab and directed the driver to her home. He helped her with her baggage into her apartment and after she thanked him and paid him, she again tended to her bruises and started to plot her revenge.

Back in New York Nelson and Dolores began their married lives. Dolores would continue working in the bank during the day and Nelson would resume his midnight tour in the post office. He would sleep most of the day but would be up when she returned from work. He learned to cook some simple dishes and often had her dinner ready when she came home. He thought about the happiness he was experiencing with this woman with whom he was so in love. A few times during his sleep Sheila would appear to him and express her joy at his happiness. He knew if he told this to anyone they would say it was a dream but it was more than a dream. He would never be separated from Sheila.

Dolores' lease on the East 80th Street apartment would end on November 30. She and Nelson wanted their own place and they had better start looking now. On the Saturday after they returned from the cruise, they contacted a real estate agent and by the first week in October they made a final offer on a house in Queens. As they were packing items away for the move, Dolores came across an address and telephone number for Karen Van Horn in Buffalo. "I think I'll give her a call just to see how things are going for her. I really liked her," she announced to Nelson.

"Let's go see her, preferably at work." Nelson said facetiously.

Dolores gave him an icy stare but she knew he was only talking. "She doesn't have anything I haven't got and you

151

can touch me!"

Nelson laughed and started to put his hand inside her blouse. She slapped him away saying, "But not now you pervert."

It was becoming the routine for Nelson and Dolores to clean up after dinner together then retire to the living room to watch television. Nelson left for work at 11:15 and Dolores would go to bed. This particular night she wasn't sleepy so she decided to clean out her purse. She found the slip of paper with Karen's number and since she knew Karen was a night person she decided to call.

The telephone rang three times and a pleasant little voice said, "Hello."

"Hi, Karen Van Horn?" Dolores asked cautiously.

"Speaking."

"Karen, this is Dolores Whitman from the cruise last August. Do you remember me?"

"Of course! You and all your friends and your husband were so nice to me."

She apologized for the late call but as she suspected, Karen was a night person. They passed a few amenities then Dolores asked, "How's your friend who didn't like us."

"That no good bastard, son of a bitch. I should have known he was a bastard.

"You know what I hope, I hope he finds the most beautiful, sexy woman in the country who can't wait to sleep with him and when she's laying in the bed ready to take him on, and he has a huge erection, HE DIES! That's what I hope."

Dolores couldn't hold back a chuckle. "What... tee hee... what happened?"

Karen told the whole story and by this time Dolores was no longer amused.

Dolores then told Karen about the suspicions about the rug guy.

"He's such a bastard, this doesn't surprise me one bit." Karen said.

"At first I didn't care what he did. I'll be honest, I just enjoyed sex with him. But after he hit me I did some checking and I found out it was only three days after his wife disappeared that he started up with me. He couldn't have been too upset about her disappearance."

"And he knew she wouldn't be found-alive anyway." Dolores added.

Then Dolores told Karen what they were planning. She spoke of the investigation and subsequent capture of Lisa and the relationship they had with Bill Evans.

"He's a good friend of ours and a great detective."

"Tell me what I can do," Karen said, "I'll do anything to see that son of a bitch pay for what he did to me and I still hope he dies the way I said it before."

They both tee heed at this and ended the call.

When Dolores returned from work that evening she could smell the meat loaf Nelson was preparing as she opened the door. "M,m,m,m, smells good."

They kissed and he took her coat and hung it in the hall closet. They sat down to dinner, enjoyed the meat loaf and the side dishes and when they were finished Nelson lit up a cigarette. Dolores had quit smoking some months earlier as she had promised. "I'm not preaching at you sweetie, but I wish you'd give up those things."

Nelson nodded and said, "Yeah, one of these days."

Dolores then told him about the phone conversation with Karen. "As soon as we get this move over with, let's get in touch with Bill and go after this guy."

"What bothers me," Nelson said, "is his checking our

license plate. He knows who we are and probably where we live. We need to clear this up for our own sake."

Nelson's only personal items, other than his clothes, were his stereo system and his television which he gave to Linda. She was of course delighted although Victoria wasn't too sure having her own TV was such a good idea. As far as the clothes were concerned they could all be moved in his car in one trip. For the next few weeks they filled boxes with Dolores' fine china and silverware, closets full of clothes and what appeared to be at least 900 pairs of shoes. All the paper work was completed on the house and since it had been vacant when they purchased it, they were ready to move in on December 1.

November, 1961 was a busy month for the Whitmans with the packing and making arrangements for the move. The phone rang and Victoria's voice came through the instrument. "You guys need a day off so I want you here for Thanksgiving."

Dolores was grateful for the invitation and readily accepted. Nelson said, "You know, it's the anniversary of Frank's death. Maybe we can visit his grave."

Since it was a very pleasant day that Thanksgiving, Dolores and Nelson decided to walk the mile or so to Woodlawn. From the house on East 231st Street to the Bronx River Parkway was all down hill but the remainder of the trip was a relatively steep uphill climb. By the time they reached the entrance Nelson was huffing and puffing and even had a slight wheeze. "I told you about those cigarettes." Dolores admonished. "You notice I'm not breathing hard." She was a bit short of breath but tried to play it off.

"O K Sweetheart, my New Years resolution is no smoking," Nelson promised.

They found Frank's grave and stood before it in silence for a while. "What a shame people like Lisa and that dude from Bradford are still alive while good people like Sheila and Frank are gone. I guess it true, only the good die young."

Dolores noticed a faraway look on Nelson's face because time had stopped for him once again. Sheila and Frank appeared before him smiling. They told him of their joy and happiness about how his life was going. "Be careful in your new home," Sheila warned. She said nothing else as she and her beloved husband faded away.

"An encounter?" Dolores asked.

"Yes but let's not tell anyone about it."

They returned to the cemetery entrance just as a cab pulled in to discharge a visitor.

Nelson quickly grabbed the vehicle and held the door while Dolores entered.

"I really don't need a cab, I can walk a mile," she teased.

"Fine, I'll see you at Vicki's." Nelson answered as he made himself comfortable in the back seat of the taxi. She stuck her tongue out at him while he gave the driver the address.

By the time they returned, Victoria had prepared all the food and the turkey was being basted for the last time. Mark and Marilyn Decker were also invited and the six sat at the table while a small table for Linda and Kenneth, was elegantly set.

They talked about the cruise, the preparation for the move, the football games and how the new first lady of the United States sounded like Marilyn Monroe when she spoke. It was a pleasant, relaxing day and it gave Nelson and Dolores the break they needed to complete the move to their new home.

The house was fairly large with three bedrooms on the second floor and an ample kitchen, dining room and living room on the first floor. The basement needed some work but could be turned into a recreation area and utility room. There were three entrances to the house, the front door naturally, a door on the side that opened to three steps leading up to the kitchen, and the flight of stairs down to the basement and an all glass sliding door to the patio. Dolores looked around and observed, "There's plenty of nooks and crannies for an ax murderer to hide."

Neither of them knew how prophetic those words were.

CHAPTER XI

THE NEW YEAR

A week before Christmas Dolores received a call from Karen. "I'm coming to New York the day after Christmas to audition for a show. I'd love to see you and Nelson"

"That would be nice, where are you staying?"

She mentioned a hotel in the theater district and Dolores asked her to come to the house for dinner when she could. Bill and Angela Evans would be in town for New Years Eve and were staying with the Whitmans. They would welcome 1962 with a small party in their new home and spend the next day at Victoria's traditional New Years Day family get together. Dolores asked, "Can you come for dinner on New Years Eve?"

"The audition is on the 29th so I was planning to go home on the 30th but I can stay an extra day. I'd love to come to dinner."

New Years Eve was a cold and dreary day. There was that indescribable smell of a coming snow episode in the air which probably would start by 10:00 PM. Karen arrived in a taxi in mid afternoon. Of course, Bill and Angela were already there and the five relaxed in the living room. Dolores wasn't even thinking about cooking that night and a local restaurant would prepare dinner for five and deliver it for a reasonable price.

Bill and Angela would be visiting New York three or four times a year so Dolores purchased furniture for the guest room. However the long term plan was to turn the third bedroom into a nursery. They regretted they were unable to accommodate Karen that evening but when the snow storm hit at 10:00 PM as predicted, they knew she would not be able to get back to her hotel. "I can sleep on the couch", she announced, "and I don't need any pajamas."

"Oh yes you do," Dolores answered, "I know my husband loves me and Angela knows Bill loves her but we're not about to have someone as gorgeous as you in our house naked!" This drew laughter from everybody as they retired to the living room.

Nelson set up a bar and Dolores put out little bowls of nuts and candies. Rock and Roll music (as well as some of the oldies but goodies) played over their new stereo system and the television was set to the network that would broadcast Guy Lombardo and show the ball drop in Times Square. The year 1962 arrived midst a swirling snow storm that did not deter thousands of revelers from assembling in Time Square. There were the hugs and kisses all around and the toasting with the champagne that Karen had brought. Then they sat down to talk. "All we know in Youngstown is there was a disappearance and we were asked to watch for the lady. Of course we couldn't do any searching. The crime-if there was a crime-wasn't even in our state," Bill explained.

"Oh there was a crime all right," Nelson said, "I saw the bastard dump a rug on the turnpike."

"But you don't know what was in that rug." Dolores mentioned, "Although, I believe she was in there."

Karen broke in, "He said they'll never find her and that she'd be rotted by now, that day on the cruise ship when he was drunk. He never explained what he meant but he had told me his wife disappeared and he was lonely."

Angela then asked, "Wasn't she from Bradford Pennsylvania? Didn't they concentrate their searches in that area?"

"From what I read, they are still searching all the way up to Buffalo and Erie," Bill said.

"She was a spoiled little rich girl and since no ransom demand was ever made, the authorities think she just ran away from home. I did some research and found out there was an auto mechanic in the Bradford area that took care of the Sharpes' cars. He went missing around the same time,"

Karen added.

Dolores : "Why would she give up all that money to run off with a mechanic?

Nelson: "She didn't need money wrapped up in that rug and dumped."

Bill: "Why are you so sure she was in the rug?"

Nelson: "Why else would someone dump a rug in a ravine?"

Angela: "Why hasn't the rug shown up, doesn't Pennsylvania keep the turnpike area clean?

Nelson: "I don't think anybody was looking for the rug near the turnpike. Everyone assumed the whole thing took place in the Bradford area. But he checked out our license plate and came in that restaurant looking for someone so he was on the turnpike. He could have seen our car from where he sat and saw us when we got into the car."

Bill: "Well do you remember where on the turnpike he dumped his old lady?"

Nelson: "I think I can find it."

Angela: "Did he recognize you on the cruise?"

Karen: "He never said anything but he refused to meet you guys when I wanted to bring him over.

Bill: "I'll take a few days off and we'll find a place where we can meet so we can check out the area."

Karen: "Has anybody considered the mechanic's disappearance?"

Bill: "I'll contact the Bradford police and mention it to them."

They all continued to chat and gradually the subject of Willis and his missing wife subsided. They enjoyed the music, danced a little and Angela and Dolores prepared some scrambled eggs and bacon for an early morning repast. By 3:00 AM they all agreed it was time to go to bed.

Nelson awakened about 10:00 AM and reached over to touch Dolores. There was nothing but sheets, pillows and blanket where she had been. He donned his robe, made smacking noises with his mouth and rubbed the stubble on his chin as he descended the stairs. Dolores was gathering up dishes and glasses and loading them into the dishwasher.

"I'll give you a hand with that, baby." Nelson volunteered. He noticed Karen was curled up on the couch sleeping like a baby. It was difficult to believe this innocent appearing little girl was a stripper and lap dancer in sleazy clubs.

The job was done within the hour, and Bill and Angela, shaved, bathed and dressed, came down. They sat at the dining room table with coffee and pastry. The sofa upon which Karen was now stirring was in full view. She looked up and waved to everyone. Dolores went over to her and said quietly, "I think we are about the same size. Do you want some underwear? I have some panties and bras that still have the tags on them."

Karen accepted the offer and went up to the bathroom.

It was very quiet and very beautiful outside. About five inches of snow had fallen and since this was a holiday very little had been disturbed. The snowplows however had been busy and the main roads were clear. There were little sparkles in the snow which indicated very cold air, usually temperatures in the single digits. This however would not deter the group from traveling to Victoria's annual New Years Day dinner. They took Karen to her hotel and after promising her she would be kept up to date on their investigation, they pointed the car towards the Bronx.

As they exited the Bronx River Parkway they could not help but notice the pristine beauty of the new snow blanketing Woodlawn Cemetery. The entire area was covered in glistening white contrasting against the deep blue of the sky. The winter sun was low and the long shadows were a powder blue. Tomorrow the cars and trucks and busses would turn the blanket to a slushy brownish gray but now, all of New York was a wonderland.

Victoria had prepared a buffet supper and everyone served themselves. Dolores sat with Linda for a while admiring her newest toy, the Barbie Doll. "This doll has a better wardrobe than me," Dolores exclaimed.

"It probably cost more too," Walter mumbled.

The men watched the bowl games while the women talked of what the new year would bring. Eventually all the adults got together and the subject turned to the rug guy.

Dolores: "Nelson is going with Bill to where he thinks the body was dumped."

Bill: "Where the rug was dumped. We don't know there was a body."

Walter: "O K suppose you do find a body. What happens next?"

Nelson: "Well, I guess we'll try to tie it back to Willis."

Walter: "Why do you think this crime-if it is a crime-has anything to do with you?"

Nelson: "When we drove past that spot on the turnpike and I saw him with the rug, he looked up at me. Later at the restaurant we see this guy walking behind our car obviously checking license plates. I got this feeling he knows who we are and if the heat comes down on him, he'll be after us."

Victoria: "This all happened before you and Dolores were even married. How is supposed to know where you live now?"

Bill: "It's not that difficult to track someone down if you have the resources and the newspapers tell us he's pretty wealthy."

Angela: "What about this Karen person. She seemed like such a lovely little lady, but anyway, what does she think? She seems to know Willis pretty well."

Dolores: "She hates the Bas..." She stopped and looked

around to make sure the children were not within earshot, "Bastard. You should hear what she wishes for him."

Dolores, again checking the whereabouts of the children, related what Karen had hoped for Willis' final minutes and everybody laughed heartily.

CHAPTER XII

THE RAVINE

Nelson and Bill both took a few days off in mid-January. They decided to meet at the Breezewood exit on the turnpike and try to find the dump site. Nelson remembered it was about fifty miles west of the last rest area on the eastbound side of the road. They met at a Holiday Inn about noon, spent a half hour having lunch and after checking the map drove off in Bill's car for the spot where Nelson saw the rug guy dumping his cargo. Bill mentioned that he had talked to a Bradford detective about the mechanic. "He told me they asked about him but he quit his job because he was going back to Canada. They believe he took the woman with him and disappeared into the wilderness."

Nelson said, "I couldn't get an investigation going with this, but somehow I know she was murdered and dumped in that rug."

They drove for nearly two hours when Nelson said, "I think it's around here."

Bill pulled on to the shoulder and rolled to a stop. They exited the automobile and walked along the edge of the shoulder. There were patches of snow here and there but in general the area was bleak and uninviting. They walked close to a half mile when Nelson stopped and stared at a small ravine filled with large rocks. "This is it," he announced.

Bill climbed down the incline and peered intently into the rock pile but could see nothing suspicious. Nelson was carefully searching the area when the heard two quick blasts of a State Police cruiser's siren. They both looked up as the trooper called down, "You gentlemen need any help?"

Bill began to climb back up the incline and when he

163

started to reach inside his coat he notice the trooper unsnap his pistol holder. Bill reached in with just two fingers, the other three pointing away from his body. "I'm a policeman, I'm getting my I D," he said.

"Youngstown P D eh? What brings you out here?"

Nelson had climbed up the hill by now and stood next to Bill. "This is my friend, Nelson Whitman of New York. We're following up on a hunch."

"A hunch about what?" the State Trooper asked.

"You know that millionaires daughter that went missing about a year ago?"

"From Bradford?"

"Yeah, Nelson here believes he saw someone dump a rug in one of these ravines right around the time she disappeared."

Nelson told about the man who checked his license plate and the couple they met on the cruise.

"So this Karen says he told her something about what happened," the trooper said.

"Well, not exactly. He was drunk and was muttering something that made her wonder."

"I'll call this in and see what my supervisors have to say. Maybe will start an investigation. In the mean time you guys better get off the shoulder."

Bill and Nelson walked back to their car. "You sure this is the right place?" Bill asked.

"I'm pretty sure, but it's too late to search anymore. I couldn't find anything."

They drove back to Breezewood where Nelson had parked his car. "Maybe the Pennsylvania police will investigate further," Bill said, "I gave him my number and he said he'd let me know."

They shook hands and Bill pointed his car to the west while Nelson turned to the east.

Ten days later Nelson received a telephone call from Bill.

"The Pennsylvania State Police called me and said they gave the information to the Feds"

"Are they going to do anything about it?" Nelson asked

"The F B I said they would look into it but didn't sound too enthused but the State Police said they'd make a search of the area."

On the first Saturday in March, the weather was nearly summer like. The temperature hovered in the high sixties and the sky was clear. Dolores and Nelson decided to take a drive on the turnpike just out of curiosity. When they reached the area where Nelson was certain the body had been dumped, they noticed some tattered remains of the yellow police tape that marked off a crime scene.

"It looks like someone was out here," he told his wife.

They had stopped on the shoulder and walked towards the ravine. Rain and melting snow had caused the rocks to move about. This is why Willis had chosen this spot. Every time there was movement of the stones, anything buried there would sink further and further into the ground. There was no sign of anything other than twigs, leaves and stones. There wasn't even any road debris or litter visible until a gust of wind disturbed a pile of twigs and Nelson noticed a fuzzy faded red strand. He picked it up and brought it back to the car. "What does this look like to you?" he asked Dolores.

"It could be one of those fringe things you see around the edges of a carpet."

"And what does that tell you?"

"That there might have been a rug or part of a rug in this vicinity."

"Let's take this to the police."

"Wait, we better call Bill first. This could be anything. We think it's from a rug because we're looking for a rug."

They climbed out of the ravine and returned to their car. Nelson nosed on to the roadway and they drove to the restaurant where they first encountered Willis Sharpe. They even sat at the same booth and kept eyeing their car half expecting someone to be checking the license plate.

They returned home before six in the evening and called Bill. Angela answered the phone. "He isn't home yet but I expect him any minute."

Dolores and Angela chatted, as Nelson poured himself a beer.

"Here he is now," Angela said.

"Hi beautiful, how's it going?"

"Good, really good. Nelson has something he wants to talk about."

She handed Nelson the phone who told Bill about the woolly strand he found.

"This is pretty thin, that could have come from anywhere," Bill said, "and there's no way to trace it to anything because we don't know where the rug came from in the first place. Hang on to it though because, who knows? Something might come up later."

CHAPTER XIII

HER NAME SHOULD BE SHEILA

As winter turned to spring and spring into summer, the investigation of the Kathryn Sharpe disappearance began to fade into the background. There were more important things to think about now.

Nelson came in from work around nine thirty one morning in August to find Dolores sitting in the kitchen smiling. Ordinarily she would have left for work by this time. "Are you all right sweetheart?" Nelson worriedly asked.

"I don't know," she replied, "I think I'm pregnant."

"Really? Why do you say that? Are you sick or anything?"

"No. I'm not sick but I want to go to the doctor. I have an appointment this afternoon."

Nelson didn't undress for bed that morning. He stretched out on the sofa to nap until it was time to go. Dolores protested telling him he needed his sleep but Nelson wouldn't hear of it. "I'm going with you to the doctor! I don't care if I never get to sleep."

The doctor confirmed Dolores' suspicions and estimated her delivery time to be some time in April, 1963.

"Wow," Nelson exclaimed, "I'm going to be a dad! Wow!"

Walter and Victoria were elated at the news and they couldn't hold Linda down. When they were all together Victoria almost had to pry Linda away from Dolores who rested her head on Dolores' lap saying, "Hello Uncle Nelson's girlfriend's baby."

"We're going to have to work on names." Dolores said, "How about you call me Auntie Dee and the baby,

Brunhilda."

"Unless its a boy." Nelson interjected, "then we'll call him Beowulf."

Linda gave each of them a puzzled look then walked away muttering what kind of goofy names are those?

"When are you going to stop working?" Victoria asked.

"I guess I'll hang in until the end of the year," Dolores replied.

When December began, there was no doubt in anyone's mind that Dolores was pregnant. Nelson jokingly referred to her as the "Hunch Front of Notre Dame". Actually she was never more beautiful. The "mommy-to-be" glow was a fact. The whites of her eyes were the perfect background for her nearly black pupils and she was as happy as she looked.

"What shall we name him?" Nelson asked.

"How about Walter, after your brother-in-law."

"I don't think so. Walt Whitman?"

"What about Blanton?"

"Yeah and we can put a sign on his back saying 'Beat me up now, avoid the rush'"

Dolores chuckled at this then said, "What if it's a girl?"

They discussed names for the next hour and were no closer to a decision then they were when the evening began. They had purchased a crib, a bassinet and a small dresser to be put in the third bedroom which had been painted a gender neutral color.

Karen Van Horn had gotten the chorus line job she had auditioned for a year earlier and was living in New York now. She kept in touch with the Whitmans and when she heard Dolores was expecting she volunteered to baby sit when needed. "That is, if you don't mind a stripper chorus girl watching over your kid," she said. Her job now, as a chorus girl was a little more respectable than a stripper and lap dancer although she was never ashamed of what she did. Nevertheless, Nelson was reluctant to introduce her to Victoria and Walter, who tended to be a bit prudish, when Karen was visiting last New Years Eve. There also was Linda. Who knew what kind of questions she would have asked and who knew what kind of answers Karen would give.

Now, however, since she had become such a good friend, Nelson thought he might ask his sister if they could bring Karen for Christmas dinner.

"I'd love to meet your family Nelson, you guys are the best friends a girl could have. I love you so much." Karen excitedly said.

Christmas day was a little warmer than average for late December. There was a milky sun shiny through high cirrus clouds and there was no snow on the ground. With several grunts and groans, Nelson was able to get Dolores into the car and they headed for Manhattan to pick up Karen. She was ready when they arrived with two huge shopping bags filled with gaily wrapped gifts. After filling the trunk with her packages and getting Karen comfortably seated, Nelson turned the car towards the Bronx.

"Wow! That's a big cemetery." Karen voiced as they turned off the Bronx River Parkway and she saw Woodlawn.

"Yeah," Nelson answered, "people are dying to get in there!"

Dolores gave Nelson a cold stare and said "Boooo."

Karen however, giggled a little since she hadn't heard that old standby cemetery joke before.

Linda was at the door wearing a Santa Claus hat, waving and singing;

"We wish you a merry Christmas..."

The trio exited the car and gathered the gifts from the

trunk.

Dolores introduced Karen and Walter while Linda introduced herself, "I'm Linda and I'm pleased to meet you."

"Hi Linda, I'm glad to meet you also." Karen reached into her shopping bag and found several packages tagged for Linda. "Here, these are for you."

Linda thanked her and took her packages to the sofa where she began tearing off wrapping paper. The adults exchanged gifts, thanked each other and showed the proper amounts of surprise and pleasure. Victoria disappeared for a moment and returned wheeling in a lovely green baby carriage. "I'll expect to wheel my niece around the parks quite often."

Karen fit right in with Dolores and Victoria even though she was closer in age to Linda. They retreated to the kitchen leaving Nelson and Walter examining the toy automobiles Linda had received. She was still young enough to enjoy some boy toys.

"Sometimes I wish we had a son," Walter said, "boys get trains and racing cars and war toys we all can use."

Nelson noticed he didn't say instead of a girl. Linda was the apple of Walter's eye and the whole reason for his existence. Nelson mused, if we have a girl I'll be just as happy as I'd be with a boy.

Walter was fingering some unidentifiable gizmo that went with the Barbie dolls when he mentioned to Nelson, "That's one beautiful young lady, that Karen."

"Yeah, I guess she is. She helped several old babes get a little when she came down to dinner in a red dress she painted on. She was a stripper in Buffalo before she got a job in a Broadway show."

"No kidding?"

"She told us she knows she has a fantastic body and she feels it's her duty to show it to the world, just like an artist has an obligation to show what he has."

"I'm not too sure that's the same thing."

"Well, she is gorgeous as well as being a delightful person and I wouldn't look away if she was nude but believe me, Dolores is the only person I want to look at, dressed or undressed."

Christmas came and went, then the New Year and soon everything was back to business as usual except for Dolores. She was granted a maternity leave of absence although she didn't think she would be returning to work. She spent her days getting the nursery ready, reading up on the care and feeding of babies and poring through name books looking for just the right one.

Nelson was extremely solicitous so much so Dolores had to admonish him. "I'm not an invalid, sweetheart, I'm better off doing some things. The doctor said exercise is good."

When they had a few quiet moments they would go through names. Dolores would mention a girls name and Nelson would counter with that of a boy.

"Anita."

"Anthony."

"Beverly."

"I kind of like that name. I am proud to introduce Miss Beverly Whitman, the next president of the United States."

"She has to be 35 to be president. By then she should be Mrs. Somebody."

"Hell, she isn't going to be allowed to date until she's 35."

"Let's get back to names."

They continued for fifteen minutes then decide to watch TV for a while.

Nelson was dozing when Dolores suddenly shouted, "I've got it!"

Nelson jumped and said, "What, what?"

"I'm sorry baby, I didn't mean to scare you, but if it's a girl the perfect name would be...SHEILA!" It would be pronounced, SHAY-LA, like her namesake.

CHAPTER XIV

THE PRIVATE EYE

They say criminals cannot resist returning to the scene of their crime. This seems to be particularly true when it is a heinous crime such as murder. Willis' business necessitated his driving to east coast cities occasionally and he would use the Pennsylvania Turnpike when going to Philadelphia, Baltimore and Washington D C. On one such trip the hair stood up on his neck when he saw a State Police cruiser stopped on the shoulder and some men poking around the area where he had hidden Kathryn's body. He drove about a quarter mile and pulled off the road. With the binoculars he had in his glove compartment, he could see the ravine with the rocks but no one was probing that area. They seemed to be concentrating deeper into the wooded areas. The weather over the past year had moved the rocks around but there was no sign of anything other than twigs, dried leaves and more rocks. He was confident the body had been buried deeper and deeper each time there was a heavy rain. He noticed the cruiser was starting to move so he opened his trunk and began poking around. The cruiser pulled up behind him. "Is everything all right, sir?" the trooper inquired.

"Yes, thank you officer, I heard something rattling around in here. It was nothing."

The policeman tipped his cap and drove off. Willis returned to his car and followed. He thought to himself, did someone tip them off? Did Nelson Whitman of the Bronx, New York see him dump the rug?

The questions ran through his head as he continued his drive to Baltimore. Finally he decided to check up on Whitman and find out if he was going to be a problem.

He returned to Bradford and resumed his act of the

devastated husband whose wife had disappeared. "You know Willis," one of his friends would say, "the longer we go without finding out anything, the less likely she'll be found. We have to face the facts."

"She's alive!" Willis would shout resolutely, "and I'm going to find her!"

When Willis wasn't present his friends would shake their heads and say, "He isn't going to accept the fact she's either dead or off in the wilderness with that mechanic."

Willis went to Buffalo to hire a private detective. Bradford was a small town where everybody knew what everybody else was doing. And besides, there were no private detectives in Bradford. He wanted to see Karen but he knew she wouldn't see him. Nevertheless there were plenty of other babes available. He found a reasonably good looking hooker and spent the night with her and in the morning he searched the yellow pages for a private detective.

Private detectives rarely look like Humphrey Bogart or John Payne or Mike Conners.

This one was overweight, sloppily dressed and had a stump of a cigar usually clenched in his teeth. He combed a few strands of hair crosswise over his bald pate and he gave off a rich aroma of garlic. Willis did not get too close to him when he laid out what the job was.

"It's going to be fifty bucks a day and expenses," the detective said.

"I'll give you sixty if you don't try to rip me off, stretching things out."

"It's a deal Mr. Sharpe. I'll start tomorrow."

Willis left the office and headed for the club where Karen did her stripping.

He sat a table sipping scotch and water for a half hour and when the waitress, clad only in a G-string and two Band-Aids over her nipples, returned for a second drink order,

Willis casually asked, "Where's Karen?"

"Karen moved to New York. She got a job on the chorus line of some Broadway show."

Willis nodded his head and when he had finished his drink, he went to the telephone to call the detective.

"While you're in New York I want you to check out a Karen Van Horn. She's a chorus girl on Broadway."

Three weeks later Willis received a report from the Detective agency together with an invoice for $1,200.00. Willis wrote a check for $1,000.00 having given the detective $500.00 as a retainer. "The extra three bills are for checking on Karen."

The report stated that Nelson and Dolores Whitman were married on August 20, 1961 and were currently living in Queens, New York. He was a supervisor at the General Post Office in New York and she was a loan officer at the Chase Manhattan Bank. He worked all night and slept during the day while she worked. They had a quiet life with not too much social activity. They were friendly but a bit aloof with their neighbors.

Karen Van Horn was on the chorus line for the Broadway show *No Strings.*

She lives in a modestly priced apartment with two other chorus girls and visits the Whitmans in Queens once a week. She also traveled with them one weekend to Whitman's sister's house on East 231st Street in the Bronx.

This last item caused Willis to raise his eyebrows. "They'll need to be watched. I'll have to find out what they know," he said aloud to no one.

Willis continued to drive the Turnpike at least once a month past the spot where Kathryn lay. He didn't see anyone poking around and the brush was growing and gradually concealing the ravine. He was worrying less and less and by 1965 he felt the only ones who might find signs of the body would be archaeologists from the 25th century. He also took trips to New York and staked out the Whitman home in Queens and the house on East 231st Street. So far he hadn't seen anything unusual. But within a year something would occur that would forever change the lives of Nelson and Dolores Whitman, Karen Van Horn and Willis Sharpe.

CHAPTER XV

SHEILA V. M. WHITMAN

Nelson's eyes began to fill when Dolores said, "Sheila."

Of course, there was no possible other name for Nelson Whitman's daughter. What is the male corresponding name for Sheila? It doesn't matter. We're going to have a daughter and she will be Sheila. Sheila will forever live in this family.

"But what if it's a boy?" Dolores asked

"It will be a girl. I don't know how or why I know but it will be a girl."

" I think you are right. I think-no, I know it will be a girl. She will be Sheila!"

There were no more discussions on the sex of the child or the name. They didn't even mention boy names anymore although Victoria and Walter asked a few times what would they name a boy. But when the answer was always, "We don't know," they stopped asking.

On that most hated day in the year 1963 and indeed, every year, April 15, before Nelson left for his job, Dolores said, "I think you better call in tonight because I think I'm going to need you."

"What's happening? I mean... I...ah...is it time?" Nelson stammered.

"Yes sweetie, I think you're going to be a daddy by this time tomorrow."

A labor pain struck and Dolores cried out. Nelson thought he felt a pain also and held her closely. "Baby, baby, I'm so sorry. What can I do?"

"Well, if you can figure out how, you can have a few of these pains!"

Nelson helped his very large wife to the car and tried to

make her as comfortable as possible. A neighbor child saw them and came to the door asking, "Is this it Mr. Whitman?"

"Yeah, I think so," was the answer.

About ten minutes into the drive Dolores screamed again in pain. Nelson wanted to stop the car but traffic prevented him from doing so. "Don't worry about it, I don't think there'll be another pain before we reach the hospital," Dolores assured him.

They arrived at the hospital and she was taken at once to the delivery room. Some husbands accompanied their wives right through to the actual birth but Nelson was apprehensive about seeing her in pain and he could do nothing. They hadn't gone to any birthing classes which were just catching on and Dolores was still a little old fashioned. She believed the father should be pacing in the waiting room while she took care of the important thing, giving birth. "It's all right baby," she told him, "you'll help me a whole lot if you just walk the floor smoking cigarettes with all the other expectant fathers."

Nelson smiled and kissed her as the orderly wheeled her into the delivery room.

"Smoking cigarettes was just an expression." he heard her say.

At 1:30 A M on the sixteenth day of April, 1963 the nurse entered the waiting room and announced, "Mr. Whitman, you have a beautiful daughter!"

The two remaining dads in the room congratulated him and he followed the white clad angel to the nursery where he saw the most beautiful creature ever put on this earth. Nelson's eyes filled with tears as he formed the word with his lips. *Sheila Whitman.*

Except for the baby, everything went out of focus and Sheila Richards appeared. She leaned over, kissed the baby and smiled at Nelson, then disappeared and everything else returned to normal. Nelson went to Dolores' room and found her weak and exhausted but as beautiful as ever. "Did you see her?" she asked.

"Oh yes, oh yes. She is so beautiful! I love you so much! Are you OK?" Nelson was happy about the baby and sad about Dolores' pain and suffering and excited over the prospect of being a dad. He couldn't stay seated even though he was holding her hand.

She answered his question, "I'm fine but I'm very tired."

Nelson still had her hand and when it went limp and her breathing became steady he realized she was asleep. He gently released her hand and silently left the room returning to the nursery. A nurse approached him and said, "I think you should go home now Mr. Whitman, there's nothing you can do."

One week later Victoria and Linda were at the house in Queens preparing things for the three Whitmans' return home.

Walter went to the airport to meet Margaret who would spend a few days with them. Nelson carried the baby while Dolores returned the kisses and hugs from her sister-in-law and niece. She excused herself and went to her room where she sat and unbuttoned her blouse. Nelson handed her baby Sheila. Dolores never looked lovelier with her daughter against her breast.

Nelson could hardly keep his feet on the ground and Victoria noticed. "I'm so happy for you."

"I never dreamed I could be so happy. I saw Sheila Richards the night my Sheila was born. She leaned over and kissed the baby."

Victoria wasn't surprised. She had been quite involved in discussions about Nelson's encounters and even though she never saw or heard anyone, she was convinced Nelson did. Dolores also believed he saw Sheila but she wondered why only Nelson had the visions. "If you have another encounter ask Sheila why she doesn't appear to anyone else. We all love her."

When Nelson returned to work he was greeted by his fellow supervisors and key clerical personnel with hand shakes and slaps on the back. He spent more than he should have on a box of cigars which he proudly handed out. Stopping after work was out of the question because he couldn't get to Dolores and Sheila fast enough. He applied for and received a transfer to the third tour starting at four P M. This way he could be home to feed the baby at night while Dolores caught up on sleep.

Dolores also was tremendously proud when she strolled the neighborhood with her bundle of joy in the baby carriage and Linda wanted to take the subway to Queens when Victoria or Walter were unable to drive but this wasn't allowed. The subway system had inadequate security and the pervert population was booming. "Can we move to Queens?" she asked her father.

Sheila Whitman was a healthy baby. She managed to survive the summer of 1963 with a few rashes here and there and a few bouts with the sniffles. By the time she was six months old she had been to the photographer at least four times for professional pictures which covered the mantle. Countless snapshots had been taken and Nelson's wallet bulged with the prints. Nelson didn't force the pictures on anyone but if asked, he was glad to show them.

Technically she was a niece but Margaret considered Sheila a grandchild and hoped she would be called nanny or grandma.

Karen Van Horn made frequent visits to the Whitman home with trinkets, toys and clothes for the baby.

As the holidays approached things were beginning to settle down. Sheila began to get teeth and was sleeping through the night. Nelson had become proficient at making formula and changing diapers although he did exclaim once, "Jeez, how can someone so small and beautiful make such a foul smelling mess?"

"You think this is bad," Walter answered, "wait until she starts eating meat."

Dolores decided she would have Thanksgiving at her house. She reasoned it would be easier for the people to come to Sheila than it would be the other way around. She called Bill and Angela to invite them. Bill had been quite busy at work so they hadn't seen the baby yet but they would be able to come. Margaret would fly in from Texas and Karen of course would be there.

The entire country was in shock on Thanksgiving day, 1963. Less than a week earlier President Kennedy was assassinated and two days later the accused killer in turn was assassinated. The baby received her proper amount of homage but then the topic of conversation turned to the incidents, the ramifications and the theories put forth. Then Bill changed the subject." I heard they found the mechanic in Canada that was suspected of running off with the Kimble woman."

"Really! Was she with him?" Dolores asked.

"No, it seems he got involved with an underage girl and took off when her parents came after him. He didn't know anything about Sharpe or his family. I believe she's dead and a lot of investigators are coming around to this."

Nelson added, "I'm certain she's dead. That guy wasn't just discarding an old rug."

Karen: "When he was drunk on the cruise ship he said something like, 'she should be rotting away by now.' I think I know what he meant now. He buried her somewhere."

Dolores: "There must be something about that area that makes it ideal for hiding a body."

Bill: "Well, we did see a gully filled with rocks. Every time it rained or snowed those rocks moved around and I suppose it would bury something deeper each time."

Victoria: "Why didn't the State Police or the F B I dig into those rocks?"

Bill: "Because they didn't think she was dead. They believed she had run off with that mechanic."

Angela changed the subject. "Naming your daughter Sheila was wonderful. Now Sheila will live forever in the Whitman family."

Dolores: "That was the whole idea. The name came to me out of the blue and from then on there was no way she would have been named anything else. We gave her two middle names you know, Victoria and Margaret."

Walter: "She'll be Sheila V.M. Whitman, sort of like Samuel F. B. Morse."

Karen chuckled as she said, "Maybe she'll invent a code or something."

CHAPTER XVI

LET'S LOOK AT THAT RAVINE

Since the beginning of time, it was mandatory a party be held for a child's first birthday, even though the child has no idea what is going on. On income tax day plus one, 1964 the family gathered for Sheila's first birthday. Dolores wanted to know why Nelson insisted on taking her picture with ice cream and cake covering the child's entire face.

At the same time, in Bradford Pennsylvania Arthur Kimble and the authorities were virtually convinced Kathryn was dead.

Willis, of course, insisted she was still alive and he wasn't going to stop looking for her. His performance should have earned him an Oscar, an Emmy and a Tony. The family tried to console him and understood why he disappeared in the Allegheny Forest for days at a time. He would go to a motel where he parked his Lincoln and kept hiking clothes and supplies including a huge Bible that he made sure everyone saw. He needed to be alone away from the sounds and sights of Bradford so he could meditate and pray for his wife. That's what the family and friends thought. Willis actually had sneaked up to Buffalo and was shoving dollar bills into garters and G-strings, sleeping with strippers, prostitutes and pickups, and frequenting every kind of sleaze joint Western New York had to offer. He had access to Kathryn's money now. He had purchased a cheap compact car which he kept in a rented garage in a town a few miles away from Bradford. He would walk through the forest to his car, drive up to Buffalo and check in to a luxury hotel. Sometimes he would travel to Cleveland and Detroit. He occasionally brought a Buffalo lady with him but more often than not he hunted down local bimbos. He decided not to take anyone away on a cruise again because you never know who you might meet. Look at what happened with Nelson

Whitman of the Bronx, New York.

He would return to the Pennsylvania garage, walk the few miles through the forest and arrive at the motel exhausted but with the serene look on his face like he had talked with God directly. He would drive his Lincoln back to Bradford with the Bible prominently displayed on the front seat.

There was a lull in crime and other crises in McKeon county for a day or two so the Sheriff would go to the local diner with some of his deputies. They were discussing the Kimble case when the Sheriff said, "There's something funny about that Sharpe dude. He's been the poor soul for too long a time. It's three years now since the woman disappeared and he comes around with that hang dog look every day."

A deputy exclaimed, "He said he was going to look for her. Is that why he disappears into the woods every so often? Does he think somebody buried her in the forest? In three years he could have searched every inch of this forest. Why doesn't he start searching somewhere else?"

"The old man told him he needn't come back to the factory because he doesn't do anything but walk around causing the entire place to be depressed."

"Two years ago the State Police and the F B I searched an area near the Turnpike," the sheriff recalled, "maybe we can suggest to him that he look there."

The sheriff called Willis and told him of the discussion he had with his deputies. Willis acted totally surprised that a search had been made but he already knew it had occurred because he drove past the place several times each month.

In the summer of 1964, the McKeon County sheriff was holding a man who was wanted in Youngstown Ohio for robbery.

Detective Bill Evans was assigned to bring him back and while waiting for the paperwork to be completed he started a conversation. "Did you ever come up with anything new on the Kimble case?"

"We were just talking about that the other day," the Sheriff explained. "Something isn't right about the husband."

The Sheriff went on to tell Bill about the long face, the poor soul attitude, the Bible he was always carrying around.

"I have a friend in New York," Bill said, "who swears he saw someone dump a rug in a gully off the turnpike. He is pretty sure it was Sharpe."

"I heard the F B I searched the area with the State Police and didn't find anything," the Sheriff replied.

"They really didn't do a good search because they believed she had run off. Now that they found the mechanic they're leaning towards the fact she is dead."

"She still might have run away, only with someone else."

The prisoner was ready to be transferred and Bill cuffed him and headed for the Youngstown police cruiser.

"Do you know where this place is on the turnpike?" the Sheriff asked

"I think I can find it, in fact I'll ask my friend from New York if he wants to come."

After Bill returned to Youngstown and turned the prisoner over to the Mahoning County sheriff, he called Nelson.

He asked about the baby and Dolores, then got to the point. "Can you take some time to meet me and the sheriff from the Bradford area at the site where the rug was dumped?"

"Yeah, I guess so. Has something happened?"

Bill told Nelson about Sharpe's strange behavior and they settled on a date to meet once again in Breezewood. The sheriff was in civilian clothes since they would unofficially be looking at the site. He called the State Police to let them know what they were doing. "I know you guys don't have the time or manpower for another wild goose chase but we have a hunch and would like to follow it up."

The captain responded, "Well, OK, but if you come up with something let us know. It is our jurisdiction you know."

The three rode in Nelson's car and pulled on to the shoulder where the rock pile filled the gully. There was new shrubbery in the area as well as a tangle of old dead branches and twigs. They poked around the twigs and brambles and could find nothing. Nelson stared down at the rock pile in the gully. He moved some of the smaller rocks around then disturbed a rather large boulder. The pile shifted and began tumbling. Nelson stepped back until the motion stopped then noticed the distinctively colored stone he had moved had disappeared into the pile. This was curious, he thought, I wonder why that happens?

"Hey Bill, come look at this," he called.

Nelson made a little pile of stones next to a large rock. He shook the twenty bound boulder back and forth and watched the whole pile shift and slide. The pile of small stones sunk beneath the larger ones and eventually disappeared. He removed the large rock and revealed a crevice in the ground into which the stones were cascading.

"What does it mean?" the sheriff asked.

"It means, there may be a larger crevice in here somewhere into which a body might disappear every time a stone is moved," Nelson answered. "If Sharpe knew about this, he might have dumped the body knowing there would be no sign of it after a few good rainstorms."

Bill then called out," I think I found something." He picked up a faded piece of material that rang a bell. "Nelson, you remember that thing that you thought was a fringe from a rug? Does this look like it?"

Nelson had kept the fringe in his wallet since they found

it two years earlier. He took it out and agreed it was similar. The sheriff said he would contact the state police and see about excavating the hole but they really didn't know where to look.

There was considerable unrest in the country in the mid 1960's occupying much of the law enforcement manpower. The Pennsylvania State Police placed a low priority on excavating several acres of real estate for what probably was a wild goose chase. The trio understood this and decided to not do anything at this time. However, the McKeon County sheriff would keep a close watch on Willis Sharpe.

CHAPTER XVII

THE SLIMEBALL

The world spins along a given course for centuries, perhaps millennia then accidentally something happens that changes everything. Supposing Queen Isabella had not financed Columbus and he decided to sail east through the Mediterranean to find India. America would have eventually been discovered by Europeans, but perhaps not by the Spanish.

San Francisco might be called Saint Olaf and a fast food chain might have been called *Sardine Belle.*

Deputy Sheriff Daniels of the McKeon County Sheriff's Department decided to vacation in Canada. He traveled to Buffalo and just before crossing the Peace Bridge, he stopped for gas. A red Cadillac convertible with the radio blasting pulled up to a pump two islands away. An obvious hooker with the minimum amount of coverage from her micro mini skirt was seated next to Willis Sharpe, her legs spread apart and Willis' hand sliding along her inner thigh. Deputy Daniels immediately recognized Willis and when he returned to Pennsylvania, he reported what he had seen.

"I knew that phony wasn't praying in the woods," the Sheriff declared, then called Bill Evans who in turn called Nelson. Bill said. "This doesn't prove anything but it shows he doesn't worry about his wife showing up."

"That's because he knows she's dead."

The next time Willis went solemnly into the woods, bible in hand and silver cross dangling from his neck, he was followed by a detective. He observed Willis going into the motel and emerging shortly thereafter in his hiking clothes. He followed him for a mile or so to a county road that led to a garage in a small village. Willis emerged in a Nash Rambler and drove off in a northern direction. The detective did not anticipate Willis having a car stashed away so he was unable to follow but he knew how to get to this village and the next time he would be waiting.

He didn't have to wait long. Three days later, Willis was in his black clothes, his bible under his arm and his silver cross still dangling and jangling. He entered his Lincoln and drove to the usual place. The detective drove an unmarked vehicle at once to the little village on the other side of the forest and parked his car where he could see the garage but remain inconspicuous. Willis arrived within ten minutes and went directly to his Rambler. He exited the garage and headed north to Buffalo. The detective followed unnoticed, right up to the downtown Buffalo Sheraton.

After parking his car, the detective returned to the hotel lobby hoping he would see Willis come out within the next few hours. He sat where he could see the elevators and the entrance to the restaurant and about an hour later his vigilance was rewarded. Willis came down wearing a bright yellow sports jacket and an open collar black shirt which matched his perfectly tailored black trousers. He headed for the lounge where he was greeted by the waitresses and the bartender like they were used to seeing him.

The detective's report to the sheriff included a women with a very short skirt who appeared to be carrying two honey dew melons in her back pockets, met Willis in the lounge. They proceeded to an adult movie theater where they seemed to engage in some sexual activity. "How do you know what they did in the theater?" the sheriff asked.

"Well I had to follow them in so I wouldn't lose them," was the reply.

"And what were you engaging in?" one of the deputies asked with a chuckle. This brought out loud guffaws from the others in the room which was stopped by a stern glare from the sheriff. After the report was given, the sheriff called Bill Evans. "We don't have anything on him that would warrant even questioning at this point, and besides, he isn't even in our jurisdiction.

Bill drove to Bradford and accompanied the sheriff to the residence of Willis Sharpe. Willis dressed in his solemn sack cloth, his bible in his hand and his ever present dangling silver cross, greeted them with, "Bless you my brothers, and may the Lord also bless you."

The sheriff answered him with, "Did you ask the Lord to bless the lady with the half of a skirt? Or the tailor who made that yellow jacket? Or the Hertz company that rented you that red Cadillac?"

"What...what are you talking about?" Willis stammered.

"Why don't you just tell us where you buried your wife?"

Willis dropped his bible and his monk like voice. "Get the hell out of here," he growled.

"We know you did it you slimy bastard, and we'll get you."

Willis slammed the door as Bill and the sheriff returned to the car. He watched them drive off and said out loud,"I'll bet that son of a bitch from the Bronx put them on me."

Willis continued his poor soul attitude but people were beginning to think he was being a little phony.Some actually began laughing when they saw him with his huge Bible and dangling, jangling silver cross. He would avoid contact with the sheriff and his deputies but if the sheriff was close enough, he would form his lips to say, "Slimeball."

CHAPTER XVIII

THE EARTHQUAKE

Bill called Nelson and told him the recent developments. "He doesn't appear much in public anymore looking like Robespierre. He hasn't denied he killed his wife, he just tells the sheriff he can't prove anything."

"Without a body, no one knows if a crime was even committed," Nelson said.

Early in 1965 the planet earth decided to help Bill, Nelson and the McKeon county sheriff to capture and convict Willis Sharpe. In mid morning on January 28, 1965 a magnitude 5.5 earthquake rocked eastern Pennsylvania and tremors were felt as far away as the New Jersey border. The epicenter was determined to be near the Pennsylvania Turnpike some fifty miles east of the Breezewood interchange. The ground beneath a pile of rocks was lifted up revealing a tattered faded piece of carpet with bits of human bones contained within.

A few hours later a young man with little bladder control pulled his car on to the shoulder and began to relieve himself in the gully below. He was a graduate student in anthropology and caught a glimpse of what appeared to be the third phalange of a human hand. He moved closer and noticed more bone fragments amid a tattered carpet. After noting the mile marker, he returned to his automobile and proceeded to the next State Police station.

He was astute enough to know not to touch anything because this was obviously a crime scene.

The telephone awakened Sheila from her nap who in turn awakened a dozing Dolores.

"Hi Bill! What's going on?"

After a few amenities, Bill asked if Nelson was available.

"He left for work a few minutes ago."

"Ask him to call me as soon as he gets home," Bill said

"He doesn't get in until 1:00 AM."

"That's OK, he can call me then."

Dolores was still up when Nelson arrived home. He kissed her then went directly to Sheila's room to find her sleeping on her back with the peaceful innocent look of a baby. She's just as beautiful as her mother, Nelson mused. He then caught a fleeting glimpse of Sheila Richards smiling at the baby and then at him.

Dolores told him about Bill's call as she prepared a light meal for her husband. Nelson dialed the Youngstown number and heard Bill's voice say, "You heard about that earthquake in Pennsylvania?"

"Yeah, I saw something about it on the TV."

"Do you still have those pieces of carpet fringe?"

Nelson said he did and they made plans to meet at the State Police Headquarters in Harrisburg.

Within hours of receiving the message from the graduate student, an army of detectives, uniformed police and forensic scientists were digging into the gully. They recovered a nearly complete skeleton including a skull with a deep gash starting at the base. The faded carpet still had stains which tested out to be human blood. The skull still had the teeth with a few small fillings in the molars. A check with Kathryn Sharpe's dentist confirmed this was her skeleton.

Nelson was horrified when he saw the skeleton laid out on the coroner's table but was able to control the urge to vomit. He gave his evidence to the detectives who compared the fibers and determined they probably came from the same rug.

Nelson's find proved to him he had in fact seen Willis Sharpe dump a rug in 1961 but it wouldn't prove anything in court. There was no way to tell when the rug was dumped or how long the body had been there.

"It's time now for my people to do some investigating," the McKeon County sheriff told Bill and Nelson. Nelson returned home and told Dolores about what was found and what was going to be done. "What do we have to do?" she asked her husband.

"Nothing I think," Nelson replied, "I'm satisfied Sharpe killed his wife and so is the sheriff but there isn't enough evidence to arrest him."

It was close to two o'clock one morning when the phone rang in Nelson's house. He had arrived home from work about forty-five minutes earlier and was preparing to go bed.

"Is this Nelson Whitman?" a strange voice asked.

"Yes, who is this?"

"It would be wise for you to forget what you found in Pennsylvania."

"Who the hell is this?" Nelson demanded.

There was a period of silence then, "Just forget about Pennsylvania and think about your family." The call was terminated and Nelson listened to the hum of the dial tone in his ear.

The ringing phone awakened Dolores and when Nelson got into the bed she sleepily asked, "Who was on the phone?"

"I don't know. It sounded like someone warning about something."

Dolores was more awake now. "What do you mean, warning?"

Nelson told her what was said and they both lay in bed, wide awake trying to make some sense of the call.

193

"Well, since we're awake anyway..." Nelson moved closer to Dolores who did not resist and gave a little giggle. For a while the phone call was completely forgotten.

What Nelson had relating to the crime was so flimsy it wouldn't even be mentioned in court, but Willis didn't know this. He thought Nelson and his wife had irrefutable evidence of his actions that could not be used as long as no corpse was found and he thought it would never be found. But who could have anticipated an earthquake in Eastern Pennsylvania? Now, the Whitmans had to be destroyed.

Dolores was resting after cleaning up the dinner dishes and the kitchen. She would be taking Sheila for her bath in a few minutes when she thought she heard a thump against the side of the house. She went to the window, cupped her hands and pressed her face against the glass peering into the twilight but she saw nothing. The house was not isolated but there was much more room between buildings than there had been in the Bronx and a hedge ran the length of the driveway separating the Whitman house from the neighbor. Dolores picked up Sheila and checked to see that all the doors and windows were locked.

A few minutes earlier, during the twilight hours when light and shadow play tricks on your eyes, Willis crept up to the house to find a weak spot, a place where he might be able to enter undetected. Turning the corner, he slipped on a wet patch of grass and fell against the side of the house. He held perfectly still tightly squeezed against the outside wall directly beneath the dining room window. It was outside the sight line of anyone looking out and when he saw a shadow on the ground in front of him he knew someone had come to the window. He remained motionless until the shadow withdrew and the light went out.

He could hear the windows and doors being checked for locks and he thought it was safe, he slipped across the lawn, hid for a moment behind a hedge and making sure no one was on the street,stepped out and walked the block to his parked car.

Dolores carried Sheila up to her room and tucked her in bed. She decided to check the bedroom window once more and looking out she saw a pedestrian walking along the sidewalk. When he passed a street lamp, she thought she saw him look up at her house. She jumped when the phone rang. "Hi Dee! This is Karen!"

"Oh hi Karen, how are you?"

"I was just wondering if I could come over tomorrow afternoon. I have the afternoon off and would love to see you guys."

"That'll be great. It's always good to see you."

Karen was no longer working on Broadway but she now had an agent and since her flawless skin was in demand for skin care products manufacturers, she did TV commercials for everything from sun tan lotion to shaving cream. When she arrived at the Whitman home the following afternoon, the cab driver asked her if she was the shaving cream lady from TV. Karen lowered her eyes and shyly said, "Yes, I am."

"I just wanted you to know I threw away all my other shaving stuff and bought yours because you're so beautiful," the cab driver said with pride.

"Oh, thank you, what a nice thing to say," Karen replied and added another five dollars to the tip.

Nelson was finishing the meal Dolores had prepared when Karen arrived. She brought a huge ball with a metal thing inside that jingled when the ball was moved. Sheila delighted in batting it back and forth and listening to the tinkle of the bell. Karen said, "I'm bringing you a nice big drum next time sweetie."

"And you, the drum AND Sheila will be here all by

yourselves." Dolores stated.

"Well, maybe not Sheila," Nelson added.

After Nelson left for work, Dolores and Karen sat in the living room chatting while Sheila continued to play with her tinkling ball. Karen was adjusting her cushion when a slip of paper with a telephone number on it fluttered to the floor. "Is this something you need?" she asked as she retrieved it.

Dolores looked at it and said, "Oh, that's just Nelson's number at work, I guess it slipped behind the cushions after I had put it in the book. It's OK, you can throw it away."

Karen placed it on the coffee table to be discarded later. Dolores prepared a light supper while Karen sat in the kitchen talking and playing with Sheila.

Willis had been spying on the Whitman household for a few days now and he knew Nelson left for work at two-thirty each day. He returned between one-thirty and two the following morning. Dolores was home with the baby who she put to bed about eight PM and then sat up watching TV until eleven at which time the lights went out except for a night light in the kitchen and a porch light. What he did not know on this night which he had chosen to murder the Whitman family, was that Karen Van Horn was a guest.

Willis crept up to the house as twilight turned to darkness. He found an unlocked window to the basement at the rear of the house and made his plans. He would slip in, wait for Dolores to put the baby to bed, then would sneak into the babies room, kill her and wait for Dolores to come running in when she heard something crash to the floor. As soon as Dolores entered the room he would smash her skull with the blackjack he was carrying. He would then bring both bodies down to the kitchen and set them in the chairs for Nelson to discover when he came home.

Willis' plan depended on everything going according to the usual routine. He hadn't figured on Karen Van Horn visiting that particular day. He didn't anticipate Sheila being restless and requiring Dolores' attention well past nine PM. He entered the basement and although he could hear voices, he could not distinguish words. He attributed the voices to TV.

Karen and Dolores cleaned up the supper dishes and retired to the living room where they happily chatted about this and that. Sheila was still playing with the ball and when she gave a particularly loud squeal, Dolores looked at her watch and said, "It's way past Sheila's bedtime. Will you excuse me while I get her ready?"

"Of course," Karen answered, then added, "May I use the phone to call a cab?"

"Sure, ask him to get here about ten thirty so we can visit a little longer."

The house was very well built and all Willis could hear from the basement was muffled voices and footfalls. He could not understand what was being said and since the TV was turned on, even though no one was paying attention to it, he heard and recognized the occasional commercial jingles and familiar catch phrases and still thought Dolores was alone. He stood near the water heater and could hear water running or a toilet flushing and after noting the time--it was past 8:45-- he wondered why Sheila's bath had not yet started. He decided to sneak upstairs and see what was going on. Just as he reached the top of the steps leading to yhe kitchen, Karen, looking for the phone stepped out of his line of vision so he did not see her. When she turned around she glimpsed a shadowy figure retreating towards the basement. Karen saw the slip of paper she had put on the table earlier and dialed the number. The timekeeper answered and said he would get Mr. Whitman.

"Hello?" Nelson said with a questioning inflection in his voice.

"Get home quick!" Karen whispered, "there's an intruder in the house."

Nelson bolted out of the timekeepers office yelling back, "I've got an emergency back home. I'll explain later."

Karen ran up the stairs as quietly as she could and found Dolores humming a song as she wrapped Sheila in a towel. She put a finger to her lips signaling *be quiet.* In a whispering voice Dolores asked, "What's wrong?"

"There's an intruder in the house, do you have a gun?"

"No, I don't have a gun, call the police."

Dolores took Sheila still wrapped in a towel, into her bedroom, locked the door, picked up the phone and dialed "0".

"This is Dolores Whitman," she told the female voice at the other end, "There's a burglar in my house." Before the police operator could ask for the address, the phone went dead. Willis heard the phone being picked up and severed the line in the basement.

Karen started down the stairs to find a weapon when she heard footsteps across the kitchen floor. She hurried back up and slipped into the guest room. Dolores had tried her hand at dressmaking and had purchased scissors of various sizes which Karen spied immediately.

Willis was still unaware of Karen's presence and didn't bother to be quiet as he climbed the stairs. There was no way his victims could escape short of jumping from a second story window. He burst into the bathroom with the blackjack and was surprised when he found the room empty. He returned to the hallway and shouted, "Where the hell are you, bitch, there's no way you can get away from me."

Sheila began to cry and Willis traced the sound to the master bedroom. He pushed up against the door which Dolores had barricaded with the dresser and a fairly large chair.

Nelson darted out of the Post Office building and found a cab. "Get me out to Hempstead as fast as you can."

"I ain't going all the way out there, man," the cabbie protested.

Nelson grabbed the collar of the cabbie's jacket and pulled it up against his neck. "Drive this f--king cab to Hempstead or I'll rip your f--king head off!"

Nelson, who abhorred obscenities, had never before used the F word twice in one sentence. In fact he couldn't remember using the word twice in one month.

The tone in Nelson's voice frightened the cabbie to where he would have driven across the Hudson river if so ordered. Additionally, the two twenties and the five tossed on the seat were added incentives. "And get on your radio and call the police."

The driver contacted his dispatcher who called the police The New York City police contacted the Hempstead police who told NYPD, "We just got a call from somebody about a burglar but it was cut off before we got an address."

They got the address from Nelson and dispatched a cruiser at once. In the meantime, the cab was speeding across the 59th Street bridge heading for Long Island with a city police car leading the way, siren wailing and lights flashing.

Willis continued to push on the door slowly forcing the barricade away. Dolores was terrified but she held on to Sheila with all her strength and prayed to God for the baby's safety. She was screaming *help me, help me* and moved to the farthest corner of the room.

A light went on in a house across the street and a figure appeared at the window. Sheila was wailing like a banshee while Willis moved more and more of the barricade and was finally able to get into the room. He was slapping the blackjack against his palm when he suddenly stopped, his eyes agape and a gurgling sound coming from his mouth. He fell forward with a large scissor imbedded between his shoulder blades as Karen stood over him with a look of terror on her face.

When the taxi reached the Nassau County line the New York City police fell back but a Nassau County Sheriff's cruiser continued to escort them to Hempstead.

Dolores continued to hold on to Sheila and Karen put her arms around both of them. They sat on the bed sobbing while trying to comfort the screaming Sheila. A siren could be heard in the distance then another and another as the police cars converged on the address. Dolores looked up from Sheila just in time to see Willis swing the blackjack at Karen. "Watch out!" she screamed and as Karen turned her head the weapon caught her just above the temple. Karen was unconscious before she hit the floor and Willis moved towards Dolores but the scissor punctured his aorta when he stood up and staggered against the wall. He grasped the bed spread and pulled it off the bed as he fell to the floor.

Nelson sprang from the cab before it stopped and rushed to the house. He had his key in his hand so there would be no hesitation in opening the front door. The police car pulled up as Nelson was entering the house. He ignored the order to stop and ran up the stairs to his family as three policemen, their weapons drawn rushed after him.

Dolores held Sheila with one hand and was on the floor trying to help Karen. Nelson rushed in tripped on Willis' body but regained his balance as he smothered Dolores and Sheila with his seventy three inch frame. The policemen were right behind him and were ordering everybody to freeze. Dolores pleaded with them to get help for Karen and one policeman hollered down to his partner to call an ambulance. They checked Willis' body and determined he was really dead.

A police supervisor entered the room and tried to make order out of the chaos. "Everybody shut up," he bellowed, "and tell me what the hell is going on around here."

"This son of a bitch," Nelson said as he viciously kicked

Willis' dead body, "killed his wife four years ago and thinks-
-thought we knew something about it. He wanted to kill us."

Nelson had taken Sheila from Dolores and held her
tightly. Being in her father's arms comforted her and she
soon began to doze. Dolores having regained her composure
then began explaining the situation. The unconscious Karen
was placed in the ambulance and rushed to the county
hospital. Because she had been warned, Karen moved just
enough so Willis' blow was less direct to the temple and her
skull was not fractured. The doctors felt she would recover
with nothing more than a severe headache.

There was a thorough investigation and it was
determined the homicide was justifiable. It was clearly a
matter of self defense.

CHAPTER XIX

ARTHUR KIMBLE SAYS THANK YOU

Dolores no longer wanted to live in this house and within a week Nelson had put it on the market. It took nearly a month to finalize the purchase of a new home in New Rochelle, New York, a semi-upscale Westchester County community. In the meantime they stayed with Walter and Victoria in the Bronx much to Linda's delight.

The day after the frightening incident, after they all had calmed down a little, Nelson called Bill Evans who in turn called the McKeon County sheriff in Pennsylvania. Arthur Kimble was at the sheriff's office at the time and he asked for the Whitman's address. Two days later a large black Cadillac with Pennsylvania license plates pulled up to the East 231st Street house and a distinguished looking gentleman rang the doorbell. Victoria answered and after the man identified himself, she asked him in. Ushering him into the living room where the family had assembled, she offered him a seat and announced, "This is Mr. Arthur Kimble from Pennsylvania. He would like to talk with Dolores and Nelson."

The others in the room began to get up but Mr. Kimble stopped them saying, "You needn't leave, I can speak to all of you.

"That evil monster from hell was never someone I would have chosen for my daughter but he seemed to make her happy so I accepted him. I never liked him and always thought he was up to no good."

Victoria entered the room with a tray of cups and saucers and her best coffee service. Arthur happily accepted the brew. He continued, "I am so sorry you had to go through such a horrible ordeal but I am grateful you have avenged my Kathryn's murder. I had to come here and personally speak to you."

Arthur arose and walked over to Nelson whose hand he took and pumped it several times while his left hand was on Nelson's shoulder. He then went to Dolores and reached for her hand but Dolores put her arms around him and kissed his cheek while hugging him. She had tears in her eyes when she said, "I'm so sorry about your daughter and you going through such hell."

Arthur answered, "Madam you are a most beautiful woman, thank you, thank you."

He then turned to Karen and said, "You are the bravest woman I have ever known, thank you."

He then took two envelopes from his pocket and laid them on the coffee table. "I must be going now and if you ever need anything do not hesitate to call on me. Thank you again."

Nelson got up and said, "Wait a minute, you didn't have …"

But before he finished the sentence, Arthur who moved quite well for a man his age, was already entering the limo by the time Nelson reached the door. The darkened window of the automobile was ascending and Arthur's waving hand disappeared.

The envelopes were addressed to Nelson and Dolores, and Karen. Each one contained a check for five thousand dollars and a note that said, "This is the reward promised for finding Kathryn."

Karen had the headache the doctors had predicted and needed to be watched carefully. She opted not to stay in the hospital but did agree to stay with Victoria and Walter. She moved in with Linda and being well off financially from her TV commercials, she insisted on redecorating Linda's room. She had twin beds put in and upgraded the room from that of a little girl, to that of a teenager. Walter was apprehensive at first because Karen was such a worldly person but Karen loved and respected this family so much she assured Walter she would never do anything to harm anyone.

"I can help Linda," she told the family one evening while sitting at the kitchen table, "to grow up without all the misinformation she would get from her classmates."

"Isn't it our job to teach her about the birds and the bees?" Walter asked.

"Yes, yes, of course, you would give her the mother/daughter talk but I might be better able to talk to her in the language of today's teens. I can be her big sister."

Karen stayed with the Spiveys for a fortnight and then visited at least once a week after that. Occasionally she would sleep in the extra twin bed when Linda begged her to sleep over. Karen explained in simple terms what was happening to Linda as her body began to change. She was growing into a very beautiful woman and Karen taught her the exercises that would help her when she was old enough, the most advantageous methods of using makeup and hair styles. When she was eighteen she was as beautiful as any Hollywood starlet and Karen suggested she try modeling.

In the meantime Karen was becoming quite famous. Her TV commercials led to roles on TV movies and dramas. She had started acting school when she first came to New York and was told she could become famous for her acting ability rather than her figure and looks. She did however, still enjoy displaying her body and explored the possibility of doing nude scenes on the big screen. She traveled back and forth between New York and Hollywood but she never forgot her friends who she now considered her family. One of the New Rochelle neighbors recognized her during a visit to Nelson and Dolores and by the next morning, everyone on the street knew Karen Van Horn from TV was visiting.

Sheila, now age six was watching TV when a promo for an upcoming movie showed Karen in a witness chair of a court room drama. "Mommy, I see Karen on the TV. Is she coming to see us? Can we go to her house?"

"She lives far away so we won't see her for a while," Dolores answered

She chuckled when she heard Sheila say, "Oh man!"

Nelson had enough seniority now to work the day tour. He was promoted to General Foreman and returned to Grand Central Station. He could spend evenings with his two beautiful ladies now and after they decided to paste pictures into an album Karen had given them as a gift. They came across the wedding picture of Frank and Sheila Richards and little Sheila asked, "Who's that, Daddy?"

"That's the lady you were named after, she was our friend a long time ago," Nelson replied.

"Can she come see us?"

Nelson and Dolores explained why she couldn't come and told her the basic story of the Richards. In later years Sheila would understand the dark side of human beings and they would go into more detail. Whenever the album came out Sheila would turn to the picture and Nelson and Dolores would add a little more to the story.

In 1971 eighteen year old Linda Spivey enrolled in the John Robert Powers academy to become a model and perhaps like her friend Karen Van Horn, an actress. Again Walter was apprehensive but he knew Powers was a reputable agency and had to admit his daughter was stunningly beautiful. In spite of her younger life, he came to know Karen, Linda's mentor, to be a good caring woman who truly loved the family as her own. Karen was in New York for the Thanksgiving weekend and was invited to dinner at the Spivey home. It would be the last one on East 231st Street since they decided to sell the house and move to White Plains. They had already purchased the lot and met with the architect who would design the new house.

As they did every Thanksgiving, Nelson and Dolores went to Woodlawn cemetery to visit Frank's grave. This time they took Sheila with them and Linda and Karen said they would go along. Nelson was now 48 and Dolores 44. In spite of them having quit smoking several years ago, the walk up the hill on East 233rd Street was a bit strenuous. They piled into Nelson's Lincoln (he had moved up from Ford models but not the Ford Motor Company) and drove the short distance to the cemetery.

They stood before Frank's stone and Sheila began to read aloud:

Francis William Richards
Beloved Husband of Sheila
December 19, 1922   November 23, 1960

Eight year old Sheila began to calculate his age, writing with imaginary chalk on an imaginary black board. "He was almost 48...no...38 years old.

Linda looked at Karen and said, "Pretty good with numbers, I hope she doesn't become an accountant, she's too gorgeous."

Nelson didn't hear any of this because everything faded into black and Frank and Sheila Richards stood before him. "Hi Nelson," Sheila said, "Your baby is beautiful and look at Linda!"

Frank added, "You're doing OK man, things should be pretty easy on you from here on out."

Nelson's eyes filled with tears and he smiled at them as they began to fade and the rest of the scene began to reappear. "You're coming back aren't you?" he shouted to them.

They both said, "You'll see us again but not for a long time."

Dolores looked up when she heard Nelson speak but she said nothing. She knew he was having another encounter. He put his arm around her and said, "I think we're going to be fine now."

CHAPTER XX

THE GOLDEN YEARS

Karen tried the movies but didn't impress the critics or the Hollywood big wigs. TV was her forte and she returned to the small screen. In 1974 she landed the lead role in a situation comedy about a single woman in her thirties who became the manager of a radio station. The show ran for nine years and Karen Van Horn became a household name. She lived in Beverly Hills now but visited the Whitmans and Spiveys three or four times a year. Nelson, Dolores, Victoria and Walter vacationed in Southern California one summer and Karen gave them the full treatment with tours of the studios and lunches at the commissaries where they met many of the TV and movie stars. Some of the actors and actresses attended the showings of the top designers and were familiar with the stunning super model, Linda Spivey. One actress that Karen had introduced turned to Victoria and said, "Your name is Spivey? Are you related to Linda Spivey?"

Walter's chest nearly exploded when he answered, "She's our daughter."

In 1979 Nelson, who had become assistant manager of Grand Central Station, retired. He was fifty-five years old and had thirty-four years of service. His sideburns were gray now but he was still a handsome distinguished gentleman. He was too young to stop working and would find some position in the private sector that would use his abilities. Heck, if necessary, he would go back to being an usher in the movie theaters. Dolores was fifty-two and was still a knockout. She still had her beautiful figure and although some lines had formed around her eyes and the corners of her mouth, her skin was still smooth and youthful. She kept in good physical shape and used the proper creams and lotions.

They didn't visit Woodlawn cemetery on Thanksgiving any more since the Spivey's now lived in White Plains. They would drive down from time to time and Sheila, a beautiful sixteen year old, who knew everything and her parents knew nothing, insisted on joining them, It was a natural thing for her to love Frank and Sheila just as Nelson had loved them and this time she brought flowers which she had purchased from her baby-sitting money and placed them on the grave that summer day in 1979.

The relationship with Bill and Angela Evans continued through the years. In 1982 the four went on a Caribbean cruise and again made friends with forty year olds and those who were twenty something. This time the Whitman's (and the Evans') were the distinguished older couples. In 1997 Nelson and Dolores traveled to Youngstown and together with the Evans' they took a two week motor trip through Ohio, Michigan, Ontario Canada and New York State to celebrate Bill and Angela's fiftieth wedding anniversary.

Linda married a doctor, twenty-six year old Kevin Jones, when she was twenty-three and continued her modeling career until she became pregnant. She had amassed a considerable sum of money and was glad to forego her popularity for a mother's role. She eventually had four children who were named, James Nelson; Jessica Dolores; Michael Francis. and Holly Sheila.

Nelson felt ten feet tall when he walked a beautiful Sheila Whitman down the aisle in 1990. Dolores and Nelson lived long enough to see their grandchildren grow into teenagers.

There were no more encounters although during a vacation in 2002, there were some supernatural occurrences.

Nelson however, frequently dreamt of his first love.

He and Dolores were watching the New Year's Eve telecast welcoming in the twenty-first century when he turned to his still beautiful wife and said, "Remember when we visited Frank's grave that last Thanksgiving in the Bronx?"

"Yes, I remember," Dolores replied, "you had an encounter didn't you?"

"Yeah, I saw Frank and Sheila and they said they were very pleased how beautifully Linda and our Sheila had grown up. Frank told me it would be easier now. He was right, its been pretty good for us since that time. I didn't tell you what he said because I was afraid it would be jinxed. Pretty stupid huh?"

Karen after her successful show, was in demand for guest appearances on Oprah and Leno and Letterman. She partially retired from show business in 1989 when she was fifty years old. She was still beautiful but had added some pounds. She made guest appearances on some shows usually in a cameo role. She was a co-host on some Emmy and Oscar award shows. Because she never married, the tabloids implied she was gay but this was not so. After the incident with Willis she lost all her sex desires and never wanted be friendly with a man. She was a little apprehensive if she was left alone in Nelson or Walter's presence. She also found that as a result of her success on a TV situation comedy, her prime asset was not her body but her talent. She was now glad she had failed in Hollywood.

In 1995 Victoria arranged a gala birthday party for Walter's seventy-fifth birthday. The entire family arrived at the party center, including their four grand children. Nelson and Dolores arrived with their three year old granddaughter, Tracy Sheila, a pregnant Sheila and her husband, Brian White. It was a wonderful party and reunion, for the family was now spread all over the country and didn't get together very often.

The following morning Walter said he wasn't feeling very well and Victoria attributed it to too much party. She went to the medicine cabinet for an antacid tablet and when she returned, Walter was dead.

Victoria was devastated by the loss of her husband and within six months she had also died. Dolores insisted it was from a broken heart.

In 2007 Nelson suffered a stroke two weeks after his eighty-fourth birthday. Dolores sat at his bedside while Sheila with fifteen year old Tracy and eleven year old Kimberly waited outside the ICU. Nelson could feel her hand and hear her sobs but he was unable to respond. Frank and Sheila Richards were standing at the foot of the bed surrounded by a bright light and what could be angels. He wasn't sure. Sheila said, "We told you we would see you again. We came to walk you home. He glanced back at his beautiful wife, the wonderful Dolores Lake he had known so well these many years, the only woman he loved as much as he did Sheila.. "Can't I stay just a little longer?" he pleaded, but Sheila said, "No dear sweet Nelson, but she will be along soon, very soon."

Dolores grieved for her husband for a while but she had accepted the fact they were both in their eighties and death was inevitable. She was grateful he didn't have to grieve for her. She also felt she would be with him again soon. Although she never had an encounter, she believed in spirits, and God and angels and heaven. She believed Frank and Sheila were in heaven now and their entry was delayed because of some unfinished business. She wondered if she would have an encounter with Nelson, or her father and mother or her foster parents.

There was no celebration of Thanksgiving in 2007. Nelson had been buried just two days earlier. There was however, plans for Christmas for the children's sake if nothing else. Dolores said she would be OK at home Christmas Day and she didn't want to spoil the children's day. But Linda put her arm around Dolores and said, "Please come Uncle Nelson's Girl Friend, please, please."

Dolores cried and laughed at the same time. "You haven't called me that since my wedding day."

Shortly after the new year, Dolores fell while she was home alone. She didn't break anything but she did sprain her ankle and struggled to the telephone in excruciating pain. She called Linda who lived in Scarsdale, not far from New Rochelle, because Sheila lived in New Jersey. "I'm calling 9-1-1 and I'll let you know what hospital I'm going to."

Linda arrived at the hospital ten minutes after the ambulance crew and found her in the emergency room. She had called Sheila who said she would be there in an hour.

"Don't be silly," Linda told her, "She's OK. It looks like a bad ankle sprain and I'll take her home with me until she can get around."

Sheila agreed but the next day she was at Linda's door before noon with an ultimatum. "Mom, we have a nice room for you and we want you to come live with us. You can't rattle around in that big old house by yourself."

She continued for several minutes telling her mother all the reasons she should no longer live alone. Just as she was about to insist, Dolores spoke up, "You're right, darling, I'll sell the house and move in with you. Thank you sweetheart."

Sheila was speechless because she expected her mother to give a million reasons why she could live alone, a thousand why she didn't want to impose and a hundred reasons why she would just be in the way of the children.

Dolores moved in with her daughter in February and was quite comfortable in her room. She tried to keep out of the way but her grandchildren were glad she was there and spent at least an hour every day with her. Sheila decided to have a party for Dolores' eighty-first birthday and Linda, her husband and four adult children were present together with Sheila, Brian and their teenage and nearly teen age daughters. They all ate cake and ice cream and sang "Happy Birthday" and opened presents. As the clock neared 11:00 PM, Dolores announced it was way past her bedtime and she was very tired. She excused herself and retired to her bedroom to prepare for sleep. She thought the pain in her chest was just a little heartburn and it would go away soon.

The next morning the pain was still there and there was a numbness in her left arm. "I think you'd better call 9-1-1" she told Sheila.

"What's wrong mommy?" Sheila cried, "What is it?"

"I think I'm having a heart attack." The word was cut short by the sharp stabbing pain she felt in her chest.

She was taken to the local hospital where it was confirmed she had a mild heart attack. "She needs to stay here a few days, maybe a week, but I think she'll be OK." the doctor explained.

She returned in six days to Sheila's house but felt weak and weary. Her room had been upstairs but Sheila converted a part of the living room into a special room through the use of those partitions that made office cubicles.

Dolores protested saying she was ruining the beautifully decorated living room but Sheila said, "Forget it Mommy, who cares what anyone thinks about my living room."

As winter turned to spring Dolores became weaker and weaker. She needed to be on oxygen now because her heart wasn't strong enough to pump all the blood her brain required. Linda's husband, Kevin, wasn't a cardiologist but he came to see her as often as possible. He confided to Linda, "Her heart is getting weaker and weaker and I don't think she has the will to live anymore."

Sheila was in tears when Linda told her of Kevin's concern but she accepted the fact. "I'm not ready to let her go but I know she misses Daddy so much."

Sheila, Linda and Kevin joined hands and bowed their

heads. Sheila began, "Father God, Thy will be done."

It was three days before Sheila's forty-fifth birthday, April 13, 2008 when a bright light awakened Dolores. She sat straight up and realize she had no pain, no weariness and she felt as though she was thirty-one, not eighty-one years old. A shadowy figure approached but she was not afraid. She reached out for Nelson's extended hand and felt reassured by the strong grip helping her from the bed. "I've come to take you home my darling."

"I knew you'd come my sweet love," she said while glancing back at her still body on the bed which was sleeping the final sleep. "Take me home now."

Suddenly many faces appeared in the lighted area, Frank and Sheila Richards, Victoria, Walter, Margaret, Bill and Angela Evans, Karen, Arthur Kimble and a pretty young lady she had never seen before.

"Hi," the pretty lady said, "I'm Kathryn Kimble. It's so nice to meet you."

END PART 2